THE MAKING OF A NATION

Copyright © 2007 BiblioBazaar
All rights reserved
ISBN: 978-1-4346-0286-2

Original copyright: 1912

Charles Foster Kent and
Jeremiah Whipple Jenks

THE BIBLE'S MESSAGE TO MODERN LIFE

Twelve Studies on

THE MAKING OF A NATION

The Beginnings of Israel's History

The Making of a Nation

The best of allies you can procure for us is the Bible. That will bring us the reality—freedom.—*Garibaldi.*

If the common schools have found their way from the Atlantic to the Pacific; if slavery has been abolished; if the whole land has been changed from a wilderness into a garden of plenty, from ocean to ocean; if education has been fostered according to the best lights of each generation since then; if industry, frugality and sobriety are the watchwords of the nation, as I believe them to be, I say it is largely due to those first emigrants, who, landing with the English Bible in their hands and in their hearts, established themselves on the shores of America.—*Joseph H. Choate.*

And, as it is owned, the whole scheme of Scripture is not yet understood, so, if it comes to be understood, it must be in the same way as natural knowledge is come at; by the continuance and progress of learning and liberty, and by particular persons attending to, comparing and pursuing intimations scattered up and down it, which are overlooked and disregarded by the generality of the world. Nor is it at all incredible that a book which has been so long in the possession of mankind should contain many truths as yet undiscovered.—*Butler.*

Mr. Lincoln, as I saw him every morning, in the carpet slippers he wore in the house and the black clothes no tailor could make really fit his gaunt, bony frame, was a homely enough figure. The routine of his life was simple, too; it would have seemed a treadmill to most of us. He was an early riser, when I came on duty at eight in the morning, he was often already dressed and reading in the library. There was a big table near the centre of the room: there I have seen him reading many times. And the book? It was the Bible which I saw him reading while most of the household slept.—*William H. Crook,* in *Harper's Magazine.*

The Bible has such power for teaching righteousness that even to those who come to it with all sorts of false notions about the God of the Bible, it yet teaches righteousness, and fills them with the love of it; how much more those who come to it with a true notion about the God of the Bible.—*Matthew Arnold.*

CONTENTS

INTRODUCTION 13
    The Rediscovery of the Bible.
    The Object of These Studies.
    The Plan of Work.
    Books of Reference.

STUDY I. MAN'S PLACE IN THE WORLD. 19
    The Story of Creation, Gen. 1, 2
        1. The Different Theories of Creation.
        2. The Priestly Story of Creation.
        3. The Early Prophetic Story of Creation.
        4. A Comparison of the Two Accounts of Creation.
        5. Man's Conquest and Rulership of the World.
        6. Man's Responsibility as the Ruler of the World.

STUDY II. MAN'S RESPONSIBILITY FOR HIS ACTS. ... 27
    The Story of the Garden of Eden, Gen. 3
        1. The Nature of Sin.
        2. The Origin of Sin According to the Story in Genesis 3.
        3. The Different Theories Regarding the Origin of Sin.
        4. The Effects of Sin upon the Wrong-doer.
        5. God's Attitude toward the Sinner.
        6. The Effect of Sin upon Society.

**STUDY III. THE CRIMINAL, AND HIS
    RELATION TO SOCIETY.** 34
    The Story of Cain, Gen. 4:1-16
        1. The Meaning of the Story of Cain.
        2. The Making of a Criminal.
        3. The Criminal's Attitude toward Society.

4. The Ways in which Society Deals with the Criminal.
   5. How to Deal with Criminals.
   6. The Prevention of Crime.

STUDY IV. THE SURVIVAL OF THE FITTEST................. 42
   The Story of the Great Flood, Gen. 6-9
   1. The Two Biblical Accounts of the Flood.
   2. The Corresponding Babylonian Flood Stories.
   3. History of the Biblical Flood Stories.
   4. Aim of the Biblical Writers in Recounting the Flood Stories.
   5. The Survival of the "Fittest" in the Natural World.
   6. In Social and Political Life.

STUDY V. THE PIONEER'S INFLUENCE
      UPON A NATION'S IDEAL... 56
   Abraham, the Traditional Father of the Race, Gen. 12:1-8;
         13:1-13; 16; 18; 19; 21:1-7; 22:1-19
   1. The Reasons for Migration.
   2. The Prophetic Stories about Abraham.
   3. The Meaning of the Early Prophetic Stories about
      Abraham.
   4. The Prophetic Portrait of Abraham.
   5. The Tendency to Idealize National Heroes.
   6. The Permanent Value and Influence of the Abraham
      Narratives.

STUDY VI. THE POWER OF AMBITION............................ 66
   Jacob the Persistent, Gen. 25:10-33:20
   1. The Two Brothers, Jacob and Esau.
   2. The Man with a Wrong Ambition.
   3. Jacob's Training in the School of Experience.
   4. The Invincible Power of Ambition and Perseverance.
   5. The Different Types of Ambition.
   6. The Development of Right Ambitions.

STUDY VII. A SUCCESSFUL MAN OF AFFAIRS.............. 75
   Joseph's Achievements, Gen. 37; 39-48; 50
   1. The Qualities Essential to Success.
   2. The Limitations and Temptations of Joseph's Early Life.

3. The Call of a Great Opportunity.
   4. The Temptations of Success.
   5. The Standards of Real Success.
   6. The Methods of Success.

STUDY VIII. THE TRAINING OF A STATESMAN. 84
   Moses in Egypt and the Wilderness, Ex. 1:1-7:5
   1. The Egyptian Background.
   2. The Making of a Loyal Patriot.
   3. The School of the Wilderness.
   4. Moses' Call to Public Service.
   5. The Education of Public Opinion.
   6. The Training of Modern Statesmen.

STUDY IX. THE ORIGIN AND GROWTH OF LAW 97
   Moses' Work as Judge and Prophet, Ex. 18:5-27; 33:5-11
   1. The Needs that Give Rise to Law.
   2. The Growth of Customary Law.
   3. The Authority Underlying all Law.
   4. Moses' Relations to the Old Testament Laws.
   5. The Development of Modern Law.
   6. The Attitude of Citizens toward the Law.

STUDY X. THE FOUNDATIONS OF
      GOOD CITIZENSHIP. 107
   The Ten Commandments, Ex. 20:1-17
   1. The History of the Prophetic Decalogue.
   2. Obligations of the Individual to God.
   3. The Social and Ethical Basis of the Sabbath Law.
   4. The Importance of Children's Loyalty to Parents.
   5. Primary Obligations of Man to Man.
   6. The Present-day Authority of the Ten Commandments.

STUDY XI. THE EARLY TRAINING OF A RACE. 120
   Israel's Experience in the Wilderness and East of the
      Jordan, Num. 11-14; 21:21-31; 32:39-42
   1. The Wilderness Environment.
   2. Influence of the Nomadic Life upon Israel's Character
      and Ideals.

3. The Influence of the Wilderness Life Upon Israel's faith.
4. The Significance of the East-Jordan Conquests.
5. The Significance of Moses' Work.
6. The Early Stages in the Training of the Human Race.

STUDY XII. A NATION'S STRUGGLE FOR
    A HOME AND FREEDOM 131
Israel's Victories over the Canaanites, Josh. 2-9; Judg. 1, 4, 5.
1. The Crossing of the Jordan.
2. The Canaanite Civilization.
3. The Capture of the Outposts of Palestine.
4. Ways by which the Hebrews Won Their Homes.
5. Deborah's Rally of the Hebrews.
6. The Final Stage in the Making of the Hebrew Nation.

INTRODUCTION

THE REDISCOVERY OF THE BIBLE

In the early Christian centuries thousands turned to the Bible, as drowning men to a life buoy, because it offered them the only way of escape from the intolerable social and moral ills that attended the death pangs of the old heathenism. Then came the Dark Ages, with their resurgent heathenism and barbarism, when the Bible was taken from the hands of the people. In the hour of a nation's deepest humiliation and moral depravity, John Wycliffe, with the aid of a devoted army of lay priests, gave back the Bible to the people, and in so doing laid the foundations for England's intellectual, political and moral greatness. The joy and inspiration of the Protestant Reformers was the rediscovery and popular interpretation of the Bible. In all the great forward movements of the modern centuries the Bible has played a central role. The ultimate basis of our magnificent modern scientific and material progress is the inspiration given to the human race by the Protestant Reformation.

Unfortunately, the real meaning and message of the Bible has been in part obscured during past centuries by dogmatic interpretations. The study of the Bible has also been made a solemn obligation rather than a joyous privilege. The remarkable discoveries of the present generation and its new and larger sense of power and progress have tended to turn men's attention from the contemplation of the heritage which comes to them from the past. The result is that most men know little about the Bible. They are acquainted with its chief characters such as Abraham, David and Jesus. A few are even able to give a clear-cut outline of the important events of Israel's history; but they regard it simply as a history whose associations and interests belong to a bygone age. How many realize that most of the problems which Israel met and solved are similar to those which to-day are commanding the absorbing attention of every patriotic citizen, and that of all existing books, the Old Testament makes the greatest contributions to the political and social, as well as to the religious thought of the world? National expansion, taxation, centralization of authority, civic responsibility, the relation of religion to politics and to public morality were as vital and insistent problems in ancient Israel as they are in any live, progressive nation to-day. The gradual discovery of this fact explains why here and there through-out the world the leaders in modern thought and progress are studying the Bible with new delight and enthusiasm; not only because of its intrinsic beauty and interest, but because in it they find, stated in clearest form, the principles which elucidate the intricate problems of modern life.

THE OBJECTS OF THESE STUDIES,

There are two distinct yet important ways of interpreting the Bible: The one is that of the scholar who knows the Bible from the linguistic, historical and literary point of view; the other, that of the man who knows life and who realizes the meaning and value of the Bible to those who are confronted by insistent social, economic and individual problems. These studies aim to combine both methods of interpretation.

Briefly defined the chief objects of these studies are:

(1) To introduce the men and women of to-day to that which is most vital in the literature and thought of the Old Testament.
(2) To interpret the often neglected Old Testament into the language of modern life simply and directly and in the light of that which is highest in the teachings of Christianity.
(3) To present the constructive results of the modern historical and literary study of the Bible, not dogmatically but tentatively, so that the reader and student may be in a position to judge for himself regarding the conclusions that are held by a large number of Biblical scholars and to estimate their practical religious value.

(4) To show how closely the Old Testament is related to the life of to-day and how it helps to answer the pressing questions now confronting the nations.

(5) To lead strong men to think through our national, social and individual problems, and to utilize fearlessly and practically the constructive results of modern method and research in the fields of both science and religion.

THE PLAN OF WORK.

These studies are planned to meet the needs of college students and adult Bible classes. Those who are able to command more time and wish to do more thorough work will find in the list of *Parallel Readings* on the first page of each study carefully selected references to the best authorities on the subject treated. For their guidance are also provided *Subjects for Further Study*. In using this text-book the student may proceed as follows:

(1) Read carefully the Biblical passage indicated in connection with each title; for example, in the first study, Genesis 1 and 2.
(2) Read the Biblical and other quotations on the first page of each study. Unless otherwise indicated the Biblical quotations are from the American Revised Version. They include the most important Biblical passages. The other quotations embody some of the best contributions of ancient and modern writers to the subject under consideration.
(3) Read and think through the material presented under each paragraph. This material is arranged under six headings for the convenience of those who wish to follow the plan of daily reading and study.

BOOKS OF REFERENCE.

The books suggested in connection with this course have been carefully selected in order that each person may have for his individual use a practical working library. The following should be at hand for constant reference.

Kent, C. F., *The Historical Bible*, Vols. I and II. Contains the important Biblical passages arranged in chronological order and provided with the historical, geographical and archaeological notes required for their clear understanding. The translation is based on the oldest manuscripts and embodies the constructive results of modern Biblical research. New York, $1.00 each.

Jenks, J. W., *Principles of Politics*. New York, $1.25. Prepared to explain the principles by which political action is governed and thus to aid thoughtful citizens both to gain a clear outlook on life and wisely to direct their own political activity.

Aristotle, *Politics*. The greatest masterpiece of scientific political thought. Its different point of view will suggest many illuminating comparisons between Greek and modern political ideals and institutions and give the reader a broad basis for the appreciation of that which is essential and enduring in the statecraft of all ages. $2.50.

For further parallel study the following books are suggested:

Breasted, J. H., *History of the Ancient Egyptians*. Clear, concise and authoritative. New York, $1.25.

Bryce, James, *The American Commonwealth*, Vols. I, II. New York, $2.00 each. Best commentary on American Government.

Cooper, C. S., *The Bible and Modern Life*. Presents the point of view from which the Bible may most profitably be studied and contains valuable suggestions regarding the organization and work of college and adult classes. New York, $1.25.

Driver, S. R., *Introduction to the Literature of the Old Testament*. New York, $2.50. A sane, thorough study of the origin, history, and contents of the Old Testament books.'

Goodspeed, G. S., *History of the Babylonians and Assyrians*. New York, $1.25. A comprehensive and attractive picture of the life of these ancient people.

Hadley, A. T., *Standards of Public Morality*. New York, $1.00. A suggestive study of the application of moral principles to the life of society.

Hastings, James, *Dictionary of the Bible*, Vols. 1-5. New York, $6.00 each. A summary of the historical, literary, geographical and archaeological facts which constitute the background of the life and thought of the Bible.

Kent, C. F., *The Beginnings of Hebrew History and Israel's Historical and Biographical Narratives.* (Vols. I and II of Student's Old Testament.) $2.75 each. Presents in a clear, modern translation the original sources incorporated in the historical books of the Old Testament, the origin and literary history of these books, and the important parallel Babylonian and Assyrian literature.

Kent, C. F., *Biblical Geography and History*. New York, $1.50. A clear portrayal of the physical characteristics of Palestine and of the potent influences which that land has exerted throughout the ages upon its inhabitants.

McFadyen, J. E., *Messages of the Prophets and Priestly Historians*. New York, $1,25. A fresh and effective interpretation of the historical and spiritual messages of the Old Testament historical books into the language and thought of to-day.

Smith, H. P., *Old Testament History*. New York, $2.50. A thorough, well-proportioned presentation of the unfolding of Israel's history.

Wilson, Woodrow, *Constitutional Government in the United States*. $1.50. A constructive judgment of the American constitution.

Seeley, J. R., *Introduction to Political Science*. $1.50. An effective example of the application of the historical methods to politics.

STUDY I

MAN'S PLACE IN THE WORLD.

THE STORY OF CREATION—Gen. 1 and 2.

Parallel Readings.

Kent, *Historical Bible*, Vol. I, pp. 1-7, 231-3.
Articles, "Evolution" and "Cosmogony," in *Ency. Brit.* or *Inter. Ency.*, or any standard encyclopedia.

God created man in his own image, in the image of God created he him, male and female created he them. And God blessed them, and God said unto them, Be fruitful, and multiply, and replenish the earth, and subdue it; and have dominion over the fish of the sea, and over the birds of the heavens, and over every living thing that moveth upon the earth.—*Gen. 1:27, 28.*

> When I consider thy heavens, the work of thy fingers,
> The moon and the stars which thou hast ordained;
> What is man, that thou art mindful of him?
> And the son of man that thou visitest him?
> For thou hast made him but little lower than God,
> And crownest him with glory and honor.
> Thou makest him to have dominion over the works of thine hands,
> Thou hast put all things under his feet.—*Ps. 8: 8-6.*

> God clothed men with strength like his own,
> And made them according to his own image.
> He put the fear of them upon all flesh,
> That they should have dominion over beasts and birds.
> Mouth and tongue, eyes and ears,
> And a mind with which to think he gave them;
> With insight and wisdom he filled their minds,
> Good and evil he taught them. Ben Sira. 17, 3-7 (Hist. Bible).

All things were made through him; and without him was not any thing made that hath been made.—John 1:3.

I.

DIFFERENT THEORIES OF CREATION.

Every early people naturally asked the questions, How were things made? How were men created? First of all, Who made the world? They necessarily answered them according to their own dawning knowledge.

The most primitive races believed that some great animal created the earth and man. In the Alaskan collection in the museum of the University of Pennsylvania there is a huge crow, sitting upon the mask of a man's face. This symbolizes the crude belief of the Alaskan Indians regarding the way man was created. The early Egyptians thought that the earth and man were hatched out of an egg. In one part of Egypt it was held that the artisan god Ptah broke the egg with his hammer. In another part of the land and probably at a later date the tradition was current that Thoth the moon god spoke the world into existence. The earliest Babylonian record states that:

> The god Marduk laid a reed on the face of the waters,
> He formed dust and poured it out beside the reed;
> That he might cause the gods to dwell in the dwellings of their heart's desire,
> He formed mankind.

Later he formed the grass and the rush of the marsh and the forest. Then he created the animals and their young.

The Parsee teachers held that the rival gods, Ahriman and Ormuzd, evolved themselves out of primordial matter and then through the long ages created their attendant hierarchies of angels. The philosophers of India anticipated in some respects our modern evolutionary theory. Brahma is thought of as self-existent and eternal. He gradually condenses himself into material objects, such as ether, fire, water, earth and the elements. Last of all he manifests himself in man. The Greek philosophers were the first to attempt to describe creation as a purely physical, generative process. They taught the evolution of the more complex from the simpler forms. Plato and Aristotle believed in a transcendental deity and found in the world indications of a vital impulse toward a higher manifestation of life—man.

Michael Angelo, with wonderful dramatic power, in his painting in the Sistine Chapel at Rome has portrayed how lifeless clay in form of man, when touched by the finger of God, by sheer vitalizing power is transformed into a living soul.

Very different yet equally impressive is the modern scientific view. The origin of matter and of life is so absolutely unknown that scientists have not as yet formulated definite theories concerning it. Even the theories regarding the origin of the solar system are still conflicting and none is generally accepted. The old nebular hypothesis is discredited and the theory of the spiral movement of the solar matter seems to be confirmed by phenomena observable in the heavens. The one principle generally held by scientists is that, given matter and life and some creating force, our present marvelous complex universe has come into being according to laws usually called natural. These laws are so invariable that they may be considered unchanging.

Even more definitely established is the so-called theory of evolution which is based on the careful observation and comparison of countless thousands of natural phenomena. According to the Encyclopedia Britannica it is the history of the physical process by which all living beings have acquired the characteristics, physical, mental, moral, and spiritual, which now distinguish them. It recognizes the gradual development from the simplest to the most complex forms. It is merely an attempt to describe in the light of careful observation and investigation the process of growth by which the world and the beings which inhabit it have grown into what they are.

A comparison of the Hebrew account of creation with those of other races and times is extremely suggestive.

II.

THE PRIESTLY STORY OF CREATION.

Note that the first and second chapters of Genesis contain two distinct accounts of creation.

Read Genesis 1:1—2:3 (see *Hist. Bib.*, I, pp. 231-3 for modern translation), noting its picture of conditions in the universe before the actual work of creation began. The creative power is the spirit or breath of God. The Hebrew word for spirit *(ruah)* represents the sound of the breath as it emerges from the mouth or the sound of the wind as it sighs through the trees. It is the effective symbol of a real and mighty force that cannot be seen or touched yet produces terrific effects, as when the cyclone rends the forest or transforms the sea into a mountain of billows and twists like straws the masts of wood and steel. In the Old Testament the "spirit of God" or the "spirit of the Holy One" is God working (1) in the material universe, as in the work of creation, (2) in human history, as when he directs the life of nations, or (3) in the lives of men.

Note the method of creation and the distinctive work of each day. The process is that of separation. It is orderly and progressive. The first three days of preparation in which (1) light and darkness, (2) air and water (separated by the firmament) and (3) land and vegetation are created, correspond to the work of the second three days in which are created (1) the heavenly bodies, (2) the birds and fishes (which live in the air and water) and (3) land animals and man. The underlying conception of the universe is that held by most early peoples. Compare the diagram in *Hastings' Dictionary of the Bible* I, 503 or Kent's *Student's Old Testament*, Vol. I, p. 52 which illustrates it.

God's benign plan is revealed by the recurring words: "God saw that it was good." What was the culminating act of creation? "Created man in his image" can not mean with a body like that of

God (for in this story God is thought of as a spirit), but rather with a God-like spirit, mind, will, and power to rule.

III

THE EARLY PROPHETIC STORY OF CREATION.

The opening words of the second account of creation, which begins in the fourth verse of the second chapter of Genesis, imply that the earth and the heavens have already been created.

"In the day that Jehovah made earth and heaven, no plant of the field was yet on the earth, and no herb of the field had yet sprung up, for Jehovah had not caused it to rain upon the earth, and there was no man to till the ground; but a mist used to rise from the earth and water the whole face of the ground."

It is possible that here only a part of the original story is preserved. What is the order in the story of creation found in this second chapter? The method of man's creation?

According to this account, the tree of life was planted in the garden that man, while he lived there, might enjoy immortality. Was the tree of the knowledge of good and evil placed in the garden to develop man's moral nature by temptation or merely to inculcate obedience?

The love between the sexes is apparently implanted in all living beings primarily for the conservation of the species, but the early prophet also recognized clearly the broader intellectual and moral aspects of the relation. "It is not good for man to be alone" were the significant words of Jehovah. Hence animals, birds, and, last of all, woman, were created to meet man's innate social needs. Man's words on seeing woman were:

> "This, now, is bone of my bone
> And flesh of my flesh.
> This one shall be called woman,
> For from man was she taken."

What fundamental explanation is here given of the institution of marriage? Compare Jesus' confirmation of this teaching in Matthew 19:4-5:

"And he answered and said, Have ye not read, that he who made them from the beginning made them male and female, and said, For this cause shall a man leave his father and mother, and shall cleave to his wife: and the two shall become one flesh?"

IV.

A COMPARISON OF THE TWO ACCOUNTS OF CREATION.

The account of creation found in the second chapter suggests the simple, direct ideas of a primitive people; while the account in Genesis 1 has the exact, repetitious, majestic literary style of a legal writer. Are the differences between these two accounts of creation greater than those between the parallel narratives in the Gospels? We recognize that the differences in detail between the Gospel accounts of the same event are due to the fact that no two narrators tell the same story in the same way. Are the variations between the two Biblical accounts of creation to be similarly explained? A growing body of Biblical scholars hold, though many differ in judgment, that the account in the first chapter of Genesis was written by a priestly writer who lived about four hundred B.C., and the second account four hundred years earlier by a patriotic, prophetic historian.

Observe that the two accounts agree in the following fundamental teachings: (1) One supreme God is the Creator; (2) man is closely akin to God; (3) all else is created for man's best and noblest development.

Is the primary aim of these accounts to present scientific facts or to teach religious truths? Paul says in Timothy that "Every scripture inspired of God is also profitable for teaching, for reproof, for correction, for instruction which is in righteousness." Is their religious value, even as in the parables of the New Testament, entirely independent of their historical or scientific accuracy? Is there any contradiction between the distinctive teachings of the Bible and modern science? Do not the Bible and science deal with two different but supplemental fields of life: the one with religion and morals, the other with the physical world?

V.

MAN'S CONQUEST AND RULERSHIP OF THE WORLD.

In the story of Genesis 1 man is commanded to subdue the earth and to have dominion over the fish of the sea and over the birds of the heavens and over every living thing that creeps upon the earth. How far has man already subdued the animals and made them serve him? How far has he conquered the so-called natural forces and learned to utilize them? Is the latter day conquest of the air but a step in this progress? Are all inventions and developments of science in keeping with the purpose expressed in Genesis 1? Does the command imply the immediate or the gradual conquest of nature? Why? Do science and the Bible differ or agree in their answers to these questions?

VI.

MAN'S RESPONSIBILITY AS THE RULER OF THE WORLD.

Consider the different ways in which the Biblical accounts of creation state that man is akin to God. In the one account man was created in the image of God; in the other Jehovah formed man of the dust of the ground and breathed into his nostrils his own life-giving breath. In what sense is man God-like? Are all men "made in the image of God"? Does this story imply that every man has the right and capacity to become God-like?

A high official of China, whose power of authority extends to questions of life and death, is called "the father and mother of his people." If he fails in the responsibility which his authority imposes upon him, and the people in consequence create a disturbance, he is severely punished, sometimes by death. Does authority always imply responsibility? Of what value to man is the conquest of the forces of nature? President Roosevelt said that he considered the conservation of the natural resources of the United States the most important question before the American people. Is this political question also a religious question?

Why did God give man authority over the animal world? Does the responsibility that comes from this authority rest upon every man? One of the laws of the Boy Scouts reads:

> "A scout is kind. He is a friend to animals. He will not kill nor hurt any living creature needlessly, but will strive to save and protect all harmless life." Is this a practical application of the teaching in Genesis 1?

If God's purpose is to make everything good, man's highest privilege, as well as duty, is to co-operate with him in realizing that purpose. Are men to-day as a whole growing happier and nobler? In what practical ways may a man contribute to the happiness and ennobling of his fellow men?

Is your community growing better? What would be the result if you and others like yourself did your best to improve conditions? If so, how?

Questions for Further Consideration.

Is man's possession of knowledge and power the ultimate object of creation? If not, what is? Does human experience suggest that man's life on earth is, in its ultimate meaning, simply a school for the development of individual character and for the perfecting of the human race?

Is there any other practical way in which a man can serve God except by serving his fellowmen? If so, how?

Subjects for Further Study.

(1) The Origin and Content of the Babylonian Stories of Creation.—Hastings, *Dictionary of the Bible*, 1, 501-7; Kent, *Student's O. T.*, I, 360-9.
(2) The Relation of the Biblical Story of the Creation to the Babylonian.—Kent, *Student's O. T.*, I, 369-70.
(3) The Seeming Conflict Between the Teachings of the Bible and Science and the Practical Reconciliation.—Sir Oliver Lodge: *Science and Immortality*, Section 1.

STUDY II

MAN'S RESPONSIBILITY FOR HIS ACTS.

THE STORY OF THE GARDEN OF EDEN.—Gen. 3.

Parallel Readings.

Hist. Bible, Vol. I, 37-42.
Drummond, Ideal Life, Chaps. on Sin.

And when the woman saw that the tree was good for food and that it was a delight to the eye, and that the tree was to be desired to make one wise, she took of the fruit thereof, and did eat; and she gave also unto her husband with her and he did eat. And the eyes of them both were opened and they beard the voice of Jehovah God walking in the garden in the cool of the day: and the man and his wife hid themselves from the presence of Jehovah God amongst the trees of the garden.—*Gen. 3:6-8.*

Blessed is the man that endureth temptation; for when he hath been approved, he shall receive a crown of life, which the Lord promised to them that love him. Let no man say when he is tempted, I am tempted of God; for God cannot be tempted with evil, and he himself tempteth no man; but each man is tempted when he is drawn away by his own lust and enticed. Then the lust, when it hath conceived, beareth sin: and the sin, when it is full grown, bringeth forth death.—*James 1:12-15.*

> For the love of God is broader
> > Than the measure of man's mind,
> And the heart of the eternal
> > Is most wonderfully kind.—Frederick W. Faber.

None could enter into life but those who were in downright earnest and unless they left the wicked world behind them; for there was only room for body and soul, but not for body and soul and sin.—*John Bunyan.*

I.

THE NATURE OF SIN.

Henry Drummond has said that sin is a little word that has wandered out of theology into life.

Members of a secret organization known as the Thugs of India feel at times that it is their solemn duty to strangle certain of their fellow men. Do they thereby commit a sin? A Parsee believes that it is wrong to light a cigar, for it is a desecration of his emblem of purity—fire. Others in the western world for very different reasons regard the same act as wrong. Is the lighting or smoking of a cigar a sin for these classes? Is the act necessarily wrong in itself?

When a trained dog fails to obey his master, does he sin? Is man alone capable of sinning?

II.

THE DIFFERENT THEORIES REGARDING THE ORIGIN OF SIN.

Many and various have been the definitions of sin and the explanations of its origin. Most primitive peoples defined it as failure to perform certain ceremonial acts, or to bring tribute to the gods. Morality and religion were rarely combined. The Hebrew people were the first to define right and wrong in terms of personal life and service. Sin as represented in Genesis 3 was the result of individual choice. It was yielding to the common rather than the nobler impulses, to desire rather than to the sense of duty. The temptation came from within rather than from without, and the responsibility of not choosing the best rested with the individual. The explanation is as simple and as true to human experience today as in the childhood of the race.

The Persian religion, on the contrary, conceived of the world as controlled by two hostile gods, with their hosts of attendant angels. One god, Ormuzd, was the embodiment of light and goodness. The other, Ahriman, represented darkness and evil. They traced all sin to the direct influence of Ahriman and the evil spirits that attended him. During the Persian period a somewhat similar explanation of the origin of evil appeared in Jewish thought. Satan, who in the book of Job appears to be simply the prosecuting attorney of heaven, began to be thought of as the enemy of man, until in later times all sin was traced directly or indirectly to his influence. This was the conception prevalent among the Puritans. This view tended to relieve man of personal responsibility for he was regarded as the victim of assaults of hosts of malignant spirits. Does your knowledge of the heart of man confirm the insight of the prophet who speaks through the wonderful story of Genesis 3?

III.

THE ORIGIN OF SIN ACCORDING TO THE STORY IN GENESIS 3.

In your judgment is the story of the man and the woman in Genesis 3 a chapter from the life of a certain man and woman, or a faithful reflection of universal human experience? Most of the elements which are found in the story may likewise be traced in earlier Semitic traditions. The aim of the prophet who has given us the story was, according to the view of certain interpreters, to present in vivid, concrete form the origin, nature, and consequences of sin. This method of teaching was similar to that which Jesus used, for example, in the parable of Dives and Lazarus. The tree of the knowledge of good and evil, with the command not to eat of it, apparently symbolizes temptation. Is temptation necessary for man's moral development? The serpent was evidently chosen because of its reputation for craft and treachery. The serpent's words represent the natural inclinations that were struggling in the mind of the woman against her sense of duty. Note that in the story the temptation did not come to man through his appetite or his curiosity or his esthetic sense but through his wife whom God had given him. Was the man's act in any way excusable? Strong men and women often sin through the influence of those whom they love and admire. Are they thereby excused? What natural impulses impelled the woman to disobey the divine command? Were these impulses of themselves wrong? How far did her experience reflect common human experience? What was the real nature of her act? Was it wrong or praise-worthy for her to desire knowledge?

In what form did temptation come to the man in Genesis 3. Does temptation appeal in a different form to each individual? The Hebrew word for sin (which means to miss the mark placed before each individual) vividly and aptly describes the real nature of sin. The ideal placed before each individual represents his sense of what is right. If he acts contrary to that ideal or fails to strive to realize it, does he sin?

IV.

THE EFFECTS OF SIN UPON THE WRONG-DOER.

What was the effect of their consciousness of having disobeyed upon the man and woman in the ancient story? Did they believe that they had done wrong, or merely that they had incurred a penalty? Does sin tend to make cowards of men? Were the feelings of shame, and the sense of estrangement in the presence of one who loved them, the most tragic effect of their sin? When a child disobeys a parent or a friend wrongs a friend is the sense of having injured a loved one the most painful consequence of sin? Was the penalty imposed on the man and woman the result of a divine judgment or the natural and inevitable effect of wrong-doing? Why did the man and woman try to excuse their disobedience? Was it natural? Was it good policy? Was it right? If not, why not?

V.

GOD'S ATTITUDE TOWARD THE SINNER.

Jehovah in the story evidently asked the man and woman a question, the answer to which he already knew, in order to give them an opportunity to confess their wrong-doing. Parents and teachers often seek to give the culprit the opportunity to confess his sin. What is the attitude of the law towards the criminal who pleads guilty? What is the reason for this attitude? A loving parent or even the state might forgive an unrepentant sinner, but the effect of the wrong-doing upon the sinner and upon others may still remain.

While the man and woman remained conscious of their wrong-doing, though defiant, to abide in Jehovah's presence was for them intolerable. Are toil and pain essential to the moral development of sinners who refuse to confess their crime? Are toil and pain in themselves curses or blessings to those who have done wrong? The picture in Genesis 3 clearly implies that God's intention was not that man should suffer but that he should enjoy perfect health and happiness. Jehovah's preparation of the coats of skin for the man and woman is convincing evidence that his love and care continued unremittingly even for the wrong doers. Modern psychology is making it clear that the effect of sin upon the unrepentant sinner is to increase his inclination toward sinning. But when a man in penitence for his sin has turned toward God and changed his relation to his fellow men, God becomes to him a new Being with a nearness and intimacy impossible before! May the Christian believe that this new sense of nearness and love to God is met by a corresponding feeling on God's part? In the light of Christian experience is there not every reason to believe that God himself also enters into a new and joyous relationship with the man? This thought was evidently in the mind of Jesus when be declared that there was joy in heaven over one sinner that repented.

VI.

THE EFFECT OF SIN UPON SOCIETY.

Men are often heard to remark that they are willing to bear the consequences of their sin. Is it possible for any individual to experience in himself the entire result of his wrong-doing? In the Genesis story the woman's deliberate disobedience would seem to have had very direct influence upon her husband. Mankind has almost universally come to regard certain acts as wrong and to prescribe definite modes of punishment. Such decisions have come about not simply because of the effect of sin upon the individual but more especially because the sin of the individual affects society. State the different influences that deter men from sin and note those which from your experience seem the strongest.

Questions for Further Consideration.

Is an act that is wrong for one man necessarily a sin if committed by another? Are men's tendencies to sin due to their inheritance or to impulses which they share in common with brutes, or to influences that come from their environment? In the light of this discussion formulate your own definition of sin.

Is the final test of sin a man's consciousness of guilt, or the ultimate effect of his act upon himself, or upon society?

May the woman in the Garden of Eden be regarded as the prototype of the modern scientist? Are there ways in which the scientist may sin in making his investigations? Illustrate. How about vivisection?

Does sin bring moral enlightenment? Distinguish between Jesus' attitude toward sin and toward the sinner. What should be our attitude toward the sinner?

If the man and woman had frankly confessed their sin, what, by implication, would have been the effect: first, upon themselves, and second, upon the attitude and action of God?

Does temptation to sin, as in the case of Adam, often come in the guise of virtue? What is the value of confession to the sinner? To society?

Subjects for Further Study.

(1) The Babylonian and Egyptian Idea of Sin. *Hastings, Dictionary of the Bible,* extra vol. 566-567; Breasted, *History of Egypt,* 173-175; Jastrow, *Religion of the Babylonians and Assyrians,* 313-327.
(2) Milton's Interpretation of Genesis 3 in Paradise Lost.

(3) The Right and Wrong of the Attempted Surrender of West Point from the Point of View of Benedict Arnold, Andre and Washington.

STUDY III

THE CRIMINAL AND HIS RELATION TO SOCIETY.

THE STORY OF CAIN.—Gen. 4:1-16.

Parallel Readings.

Hist. Bible, Vol. 1, 42-46.
Jenks, Prin. of Pol. 1-16.
August Drahms, The Criminal.

Now in the course of time it came to pass, that Cain brought some of the fruit of the ground as an offering to Jehovah. And Abel also brought some of the firstlings of his flock and of their fat. And Jehovah looked favorably upon Abel and his offering: but for Cain and his offering he had no regard.

Therefore, Cain was very angry and his countenance fell. And Jehovah said to Cain,

> Why art thou angry?
> And why is thy countenance fallen?
> If thou doest well, is there not acceptance?
> But if thou doest not well,
> Does not sin crouch at the door?
> And to thee shall be its desire,
> But thou shouldst rule over it.

Then Cain said to Abel his brother, Let us go into the field. And while they were in the field, Cain rose up against Abel his brother and slew him.

And when Jehovah said to Cain, Where is Abel thy brother? he said, I, know not; am I my brother's keeper.—Gen. 4:3-9 *(Hist. Bible)*.

And the Scribes and the Pharisees bring a woman taken in adultery; and having set her in the midst, they say unto Jesus, Teacher, this woman hath been taken in adultery, in the very act. Now in the law Moses commanded us to stone such: what then sayest thou of her? And this they said trying him, that they might have whereof to accuse him. But Jesus stooped down and with his finger wrote on the ground. And when they continued asking him, he lifted himself, and said unto them, He that is without sin among you, let him first cast a stone at her. And again he stooped down and with his finger wrote on the ground. And they, when they heard it, went out one by one, beginning from the eldest, even unto the last: and Jesus was left alone, and the woman, where she was, in the midst. And Jesus lifted himself up and said unto her, Woman, where are they? Did no man condemn thee? And she said, No man, Lord. And Jesus said, Neither do I condemn thee. Go thy way; from henceforth sin no more.—*John 8:3-11*.

Every experiment by multitudes or individuals that has a sensual or selfish aim will fail.—*Emerson*.

When you meet one of these men or women be to them a Divine man; be to them thought and virtue; let their timid aspirations find in you a friend; let their trampled instincts be genially tempted out in your atmosphere; let their doubts know that you have doubted, and their wonder feel that you have wondered.—*Emerson*.

But I still have a good heart and believe in myself and fellow men and the God who made us all.—*Robert Louis Stevenson*.

I.

THE MEANING OF THE STORY OF CAIN.

In Arabia and Palestine to-day, as in the past, a man's prosperity or misfortune is universally regarded as the evidence of divine approval or disapproval. Even Jesus' disciples on seeing a blind man by the wayside, raised the question: "Did this man sin or his parents?" Among the Arabs of the desert the tribal mark, either tattooing or a distinctive way of cutting the hair, insures the powerful protection of the tribe. Each tribesman is under the most sacred obligation to protect the life of a member of his tribe, or to avenge, if need be with his own life-blood, every injury done him. Without the tribal mark a man becomes an outlaw. Many scholars, therefore, think that the mark placed upon Cain was not primarily a stigma proclaiming his guilt, but rather a token that protected him from violence at the hands of Jehovah's people and compelled them to avenge any wrongs that might befall him.

In the light of these facts would it not seem possible that Cain's character and conduct are the reason why his offering was not accepted?

What is the meaning and purpose of Jehovah's question, Where is Abel thy brother? Is it probable that in the question, Am I my brother's keeper, the writer intended to assert the responsibility of society for the acts of its members? In China where to-day, far more than in the West, there exists the responsibility of neighbors, those who fail to exert the proper influence over the character and conduct of a criminal neighbor often have their houses razed to the ground and the sites sown with salt. Is society responsible for producing criminals? How far am I personally responsible for my neighbor's acts?

II.

THE MAKING OF A CRIMINAL.

Paul said, "All men have sinned." Are all men therefore criminals? What constitutes a criminal? Was Cain a criminal before he slew his brother? Legally? Morally?

Was Cain's motive in the worship of God truly religious or merely mercenary? This portrait of Cain illustrates the fact that formal religious worship does not necessarily deter a man from becoming a criminal. Sometimes men prominent in religious work become defaulters or commit other crimes. Does this story suggest the fundamental reason why great crimes are sometimes committed by religious leaders? The motive rather than the form is clearly the one thing absolutely essential in religious worship.

Was the slaying of Abel the result simply of jealousy or a sudden fit of anger or of a gradual deterioration of character? Compare the gradual development of the criminal instincts in Shakespeare's Macbeth. Think of the different influences tending to make criminals! Most criminals are made before they reach the age of twenty-one. The development of the criminal is the result either of wrong education or the lack of right education. Parents by their failure to guard carefully their children's associates and to develop in them habits of self-control, respect for the rights of others, and a sense of social and civic obligation, are perhaps more than any other class responsible for the growth of criminals. In what ways does the State through its negligence also contribute to the making of criminals?

III.

THE CRIMINAL'S ATTITUDE TOWARDS SOCIETY.

Every criminal act is anti-social. Few if any criminals realize this fact. A superintendent of the Elmira Reformatory after years of experience said that he had never seen a criminal who felt remorse; while criminals usually regretted being caught, they always excused their crime. The criminal repudiates his social obligations, not acknowledging the fact that the basis of all society is the recognition of the rights of others. The thief often excuses his acts by asserting that society owes him a living. Is this position right or do you agree with the following statement? "The criterion of what is for the benefit of the community at large must be settled by the community itself, not by an individual. The citizen, then, may and must do what the community determines it is best for him to do; he must stand in the forefront of battle if so ordered. He must not do what the State forbids; he may be deprived of liberty and life if he does."—*Jenks.*

IV.

THE WAYS IN WHICH
SOCIETY DEALS WITH THE CRIMINAL.

Cain's punishment was banishment rather than imprisonment. What was the fate that Cain specially feared? Cain and Abel in the original story, some writers believe, represented tribes (see *Hist. Bible*, I, 44). Among nomadic peoples in the early East, as to-day, the punishment of murder was left to the family or tribe of the murdered man. Was this just or effective? The same crude method of avenging wrongs is found in the vendetta of Italy and the family feuds in certain sparsely settled regions in the United States. The survival of this institution is to-day one of the greatest obstacles to civilization in those regions. Why?

In most criminal legislation the chief emphasis is placed on punishment. For example, thieves are punished with imprisonment. Why? A radical change in public opinion is now taking place. The prevailing method of dealing with crimes advocated by penologists to-day is the protection of society if possible by the reform of the criminal. Does this method protect society effectually? Why is it that criminals generally prefer a definite term in prison rather than an indefinite sentence with the possibility of release in less than half the time? Which method of treatment is best in the end for the wrong-doer?

It is important to distinguish clearly between the private and the official attitude toward the criminal. As individuals, who cannot know the motives, we should heed the maxim of Jesus: "Judge not!" As public officials whose duty it is to protect society, we are under obligation to deal firmly and effectively with the criminal. What would probably have been the result had Cain confessed his crime? God was far more lenient even with the unrepentant Cain than were his fellow men. Did God, however, remit Cain's sentence? Cain said, "I shall become a fugitive and a wanderer on the face of the earth." Was this sense of being an outcast the most painful element in Cain's punishment? All crime thus in a sense brings its own punishment. If in placing upon Cain a tribal mark, thereby protecting him from being killed, God apparently aimed to give him an opportunity to reform, the clear implication is that the divine love and care still follow him. That love and that care never cease toward even the most depraved. Compare Jesus' attitude toward the criminal, as illustrated in his ministry and especially in his dealing with the woman taken in adultery. His forgiveness of the woman's sin did not cancel the social results, but gave her a new basis for right living in the future. She realized that some one believed in her. Is this one of the most important influences to-day in assisting weak men and in redeeming criminals? Henry Drummond when asked the secret of his success with men said, "I love men."

V.

HOW TO DEAL WITH CRIMINALS.

The purpose of criminal legislation and administration is clearly the protection of society. The criminals are punished, not for the mere sake of the punishment or for vengeance, but to deter them from further crime or to serve as a warning to others. Only on this account can punishment be justified.

To prove an effective warning the punishment for crime should be certain, prompt and just. For these reasons effective police, upright judges and fair methods of procedure are absolutely essential. Efforts should be made not to influence the courts by public opinion, and the pernicious prejudgment of cases by popular newspapers should be discountenanced.

The surest method of stopping a criminal's dangerous activity is to reform him; to give him a new and absorbing interest. Experience at our best reformatories shows that with the indeterminate sentence a very large majority of young criminals can be transformed into safe and useful citizens. This method is both cheaper and more effective than direct punishment for fixed terms.

VI.

THE PREVENTION OF CRIME.

The best method of dealing with crime is that of prevention. The work of protecting society against crime should begin with arousing parents to the sense of their responsibilities and by training them thoroughly in the duties of parenthood. Philanthropic agencies, the church, the schools, the State, may do much both by training character and by removing temptation. The maintenance of good economic conditions, provision for wholesome amusements, improved sanitation, all tend to remove pernicious influences and strengthen the power of resistance to temptation. The public press and the theatre, which are at times exceedingly harmful agencies, may be and should be transformed into active moral forces. In furthering all these reform measures and preventive movements each individual has a personal responsibility, and, as an active citizen, he may render most important service. The home, the school, the church and the State, all touch the individual on every side and create and together control the influences that make or unmake character.

Questions for Further Consideration.

What was the effect of Cain's anger upon his own life?

Gladstone said, "I do not have time to hate anybody."

In what way do anger and hatred hamper one's greatest usefulness? Do you believe in the modern theories regarding the effect of jealousy and hatred upon the body?

Is capital punishment at times a necessity?

What is the most effective argument which can be used to restore honor and manhood to a criminal?

Is there any particular agency at work in your community to assist men who have committed crimes?

Is the chief object of punishment to avenge the wrong, to punish the criminal, to deter others from committing similar crimes, or to reclaim the wrong-doer?

Subjects for Further Study.

(1) The Effect of the Semitic Law of Blood-revenge upon *(a)* the criminal, *(b)* society and *(c)* possible criminals. Kent, *Israel's Laws and Legal Precedents*, 91, 114-116; Smith, *Religion of the Semites*, 72, 420.

(2) Mrs. Ballington Booth's Work for Released Prisoners. *After Prison—What?*
(3) The Practical Effects of the Indeterminate Sentence. Reports of the Prison Reform Association.
(4) Influence of Contract Prison Labor. American Magazine, 1912, Jan., Feb., Mar., April.

STUDY IV

THE SURVIVAL OF THE FITTEST.

THE STORY OF THE GREAT FLOOD.—
Gen. 6-8.

Parallel Readings.

Hist. Bible I, 52-65.
Darwin, Origin of Species; Wallace, Darwinism; 3. William
    Dawson, Modern Ideas of Evolution; Article
    Evolution in leading encyclopedias.

When Jehovah saw that the wickedness of man was great in the earth, and that every purpose in the thoughts of his heart was only evil continually, it was a source of regret that he had made man on the earth and it grieved him to his heart. Therefore Jehovah said, I will destroy from the face of the ground man whom I have created, for I regret that I have made mankind.

Then Jehovah said to Noah, enter thou and all thy house into the ark; for thee I have found righteous before me in this generation.

And Noah did according to all that Jehovah commanded him.

Then Jehovah destroyed everything that existed upon the face of the ground, both man and animals, and creeping things, and birds of the heavens, so that they were destroyed from the earth;

and Noah only was left and they who were with him in the ark.—Gen. 6:5-8; 7:1, 5, 23 *(Hist. Bible)*.

And without faith it is impossible to be well-pleasing with God; for he that cometh to God must believe that he is, and that he is a rewarder of them that seek after him. By faith Noah, being warned of God concerning things not seen as yet, moved with godly fear, prepared an ark to the saving of his house, through which he condemned the world and became heir of the righteousness which is according to faith.—*Heb. 11:6, 7*.

Rare is the man who can look back over his life and not confess, at least to himself, that the things which have made him most a man are the very things from which he tried with all his soul to escape.

> If we would attain happiness,
> We must first attain helpfulness.

> But stay! no age was e'er degenerate
> Unless men held it at too cheap a rate,
> For in our likeness still we shape our fate.
> —Lowell.

I.

THE TWO BIBLICAL ACCOUNTS OF THE FLOOD.

Careful readers of Genesis 6-9 have long recognized certain difficulties in interpreting the narrative as it now stands. Thus, for example, in 6:20 Noah is commanded to take into the ark two of every kind of beast and bird; but in 7:2, 3 he is commanded to take in seven of all the clean beasts and birds. According to 7:4, 12 the flood came as the result of a forty days' rain; but according to 7:11 it was because the fountains of the great deep were broken up and the windows of heaven were opened. Again, according to 7:17, the flood continued on the earth forty days; while according to 7:24 its duration was a hundred and fifty days.

These fundamental variations and the presence of duplicate versions of the same incidents point, some writers think, to two originally distinct accounts of the flood which have been closely woven together by the final editor of the book of Genesis. When these two accounts are disentangled, they are each practically complete and apparently represent variant versions of the same flood story. (See *Hist. Bible*, I, 53-56, for these two parallel accounts.) The one, known as the prophetic version, was written, these writers believe, about 650 B.C. It has the flowing, vivid, picturesque, literary style and the point of view of the prophetic teacher. In this account the number seven prevails. Seven of each clean beast and bird are taken into the ark to provide food for Noah and his family. Seven days the waters rose, and at intervals of seven days he sent out a raven and a dove. The flood from its beginning to the time when Noah disembarked continued sixty-eight days. At the end, when he had determined by sending out birds that the waters had subsided, he went forth from the ark and reared an altar and offered sacrifice to Jehovah of every clean beast and bird.

The other and more detailed account is apparently the sequel of the late priestly narratives found in Genesis 1 and 5. The style is that of a legal writer—formal, exact and repetitious. In this account only two of each kind of beast and bird are taken into the ark. The flood lasts for over a year and is universal, covering even the tops of the highest mountains. No animals are sacrificed, for according to the priestly writer this custom was first instituted by Moses. When the flood subsides, however, a covenant is concluded and is sealed by the rainbow in accordance with which man's commission to rule over all other living things is renewed and divine permission is given to each to eat of the flesh of animals, provided only that men carefully abstain from eating the blood. This later account is dated by this group of modern Biblical scholars about 400 B.C.

II.

THE CORRESPONDING BABYLONIAN FLOOD STORIES.

Closely parallel to these two variant Biblical accounts of the flood are the two Babylonian versions, which have fortunately been almost wholly recovered. The older Babylonian account is found in the eleventh tablet of the Gilgamesh epic, which comes from the library of Asshurbanipal. This great conqueror lived contemporaneously with Manasseh during whose reign Assyrian influence was paramount in the kingdom of Judah. In his quest for healing and immortality Gilgamesh reached the abode of the Babylonian hero of the flood. In response to Gilgamesh's question as to how he, a mortal, attained immortality the Babylonian Noah recounts the story of the flood. It was brought about by the Babylonian gods in order to destroy the city of Shurippak, situated on the banks of the Euphrates. The god Ea gave the warning to his worshipper, the hero of the flood, and commanded him:

> Construct a house, build a ship,
> Leave goods, look after life,
> Forsake possessions, and save life,
> Cause all kinds of living things to go up into the ship.
> The ship which thou shalt build,—
> Exact shall be its dimensions:
> Its breadth shall equal its length;
> On the great deep launch it.
> I understood and said to Ea, my lord:
> "Behold, my lord, what thou hast commanded,
> I have reverently received and will carry out."

A detailed account then follows of the building of the ark. Its dimensions were one hundred and twenty cubits in each direction. It was built in six stories, each of which was divided into nine parts. Plentiful provisions were next carried on board and a great feast was held to commemorate the completion of the ark. After carrying on board his treasures of silver and gold he adds:

> All the living creatures of all kinds I loaded on it.
> I brought on board my family and household;
> Cattle of the field, beasts of the field, the craftsmen,
> All of them I brought on board.

In the evening at the command of the god Shamash the rains began to descend. Then the Babylonian Noah entered the ship and closed the door and entrusted the great house with its contents to the captain. The description of the tempest that follows is exceedingly vivid and picturesque.

When the first light of dawn shone forth,
There rose from the horizon a dark cloud, within which
    Adad thundered,
Nabu and Marduk marched at the front,
The heralds passed over mountains and land;
Nergal tore out the ship's mast,
Ninib advanced, following up the attack,
The spirits of earth raised torches,
With their sheen they lighted up the world.
Adad's tempest reached to heaven,
And all light was changed to darkness.
So great was the havoc wrought by the storm that
The gods bowed down, sat there weeping,
Close pressed together were their lips.

For six days and nights the storm raged, but on the seventh day it subsided and the flood began to abate. Of the race of mortals, however, every voice was hushed. At last the ship approached the mountain Nisir which lay on the northern horizon, as viewed from the Tigris-Euphrates valley. Here the ship grounded. Then,

When the seventh day arrived,
I sent forth a dove and let it loose,
The dove went forth, but came back;
Because it found no resting-place, it returned:
Then I sent forth a swallow, but it came back;
Because it found no resting-place, it returned.
Then I sent forth a raven and let it loose,
The raven went forth and saw that the waters had
    decreased;
It fed, it waded, it croaked, but did not return.
Then I sent forth everything in all directions, and offered
    a sacrifice,
I made an offering of incense on the highest peak of the
    mountain,
Seven and seven bowls I placed there,
And over them I poured out calamus, cedar wood and
    fragrant herbs.
The gods inhaled the odor,

> The gods inhaled the sweet odor,
> The gods gathered like flies above the sacrifice.

At the intercession of Ea, the Babylonian Noah and his wife were granted immortality and permitted "to dwell in the distance at the confluence of the streams."

A later version of the same Babylonian flood story is quoted by Eusebius from the writings of the Chaldean priest Berossus who lived about the fourth century B.C. According to this version the god Kronos appeared in a dream to Xisuthros, the hero, who, like Noah in the priestly account, was the last of the ten ancient Babylonian kings. At the command of the god he built a great ship fifteen stadia long and two in width. Into this he took not only his family and provisions, but quadrupeds and birds of all kinds. When the flood began to recede, he sent out a bird, which quickly returned. After a few days he sent forth another bird, which returned with mud on its feet. When the third bird failed to return, he took off the cover of the ship and found that it had stranded on a mountain of Armenia. The mountain in the Biblical account is identified with Mount Ararat. Disembarking, the Babylonian Noah kissed the earth and, after building an altar, offered a sacrifice to the gods.

Thus the variations between the older and later Babylonian accounts of the flood correspond in general to those that have been already noted in the Biblical versions. Which Biblical account does the earliest Babylonian narrative resemble most closely? In what details do they agree? Are these coincidences merely accidental or do they point possibly to a common tradition? How far do the later Biblical and Babylonian accounts agree? What is the significance of these points of agreement?

III.

HISTORY OF THE BIBLICAL FLOOD STORIES.

On the basis of the preceding comparisons some writers attempt to trace tentatively the history of the flood tradition current among the peoples of southwestern Asia. A fragment of the Babylonian flood story, coming from at least as early as 2000 B.C., has recently been discovered. The probability is that the tradition goes back to the earliest beginnings of Babylonian history. The setting of the Biblical accounts of the flood is also the Tigris-Euphrates valley rather than Palestine. The description of the construction of the ark in Genesis 6:14-16 is not only closely parallel to that found in the Babylonian account, but the method—the smearing of the ark within and without with bitumen—is peculiar to the Tigris-Euphrates valley. Many scholars believe, therefore, that Babylonia was the original home of the Biblical flood story.

Its exact origin, however, is not so certain. Many of its details were doubtless suggested by the annual floods and fogs which inundate that famous valley and recall the primeval chaos so vividly pictured in the corresponding Babylonian story of the creation. It may have been based on the remembrances of a great local inundation, possibly due to the subsidence of great areas of land. In the earliest Hebrew records there is no trace of this tradition, although it may have been known to the Aramean ancestors of the Hebrews. The literary evidence, however, suggests that it was first brought to Palestine by the Assyrians. During the reactionary reign of Manasseh, Assyrian customs and Baylonian ideas, which these conquerors had inherited, inundated Judah. Even in the temple at Jerusalem the Babylonians' gods, the host of heaven, were worshipped by certain of the Hebrews. The few literary inscriptions which come from this period, those found in the mound at Gezer, are written in the Assyrian script and contain the names of Assyrian officials.

Later when the Jewish exiles were carried to Babylonia, they naturally came into contact again with the Babylonian account of the flood, but in its later form, as the comparisons already instituted clearly indicate. It is thus possible, these scholars believe, to trace, in outline at least, the literary history of the Semitic flood story in its various transformations through a period of nearly two thousand years.

IV.

AIM OF THE BIBLICAL WRITERS IN RECOUNTING THE FLOOD STORY.

The practical question which at once suggests itself is, What place or right has this ancient Semitic tradition, if such it is, among the Biblical narratives? At best the historical data which it preserves are exceedingly small and of doubtful value. Is it possible that the prophetic and priestly historians found these stories on the lips of the people and sought in this heroic way to divest them of their polytheistic form and, in certain respects, immoral implications? A minute comparison of the Babylonian and Biblical accounts indicates that this may perhaps be precisely what has been done; but the majestic, just God of the Biblical narratives is far removed from the capricious, intriguing gods of the Babylonian tradition, who hang like flies over the battlements of heaven, stupefied with terror because of the destruction which they had wrought.

Each of the Biblical narrators seems to be seeking also by means of these illustrations to teach certain universal moral and religious truths. In this respect the two variant Biblical narratives are in perfect agreement. The destruction of mankind came not as the fiat of an arbitrary Deity, but because of the purpose which God had before him in the work of creation, and because that purpose was good. Men by their sins and wilful failure to observe his benign laws were thwarting that purpose. Hence in accord with the just laws of the universe their destruction was unavoidable, and it came even as effect follows cause. On the other hand, these ancient teachers taught with inimitable skill that God would not destroy that which was worthy of preservation.

In each of the accounts the character of Noah stands in striking contrast with those of his contemporaries. The story as told is not merely an illustration of the truth that righteousness brings its just reward, but of the profounder principle that it is the morally fit who survive. In both of the versions Noah in a very true sense represents the beginning of a new creation: he is the traditional father of a better race. To him are given the promises which God was eager to realize in the life of humanity. In the poetic fancy of the ancient East even the resplendent rainbow, which proclaimed the return of the sun after the storm, was truly interpreted as evidence of God's fatherly love and care for his children. In the light of these profound religious teachings may any one reasonably question the right of these stories to a place in the Bible? Did not Jesus himself frequently use illustrations drawn from earlier history or from nature to make clear his teachings? Is it not evidence of superlative teaching skill to use that which is familiar and, therefore, of interest to those taught, in order to inculcate the deeper moral and religious truths of life?

V.

SURVIVAL OF THE FITTEST IN THE NATURAL WORLD.

It is interesting and illuminating to note how the ancient Hebrew prophets in their religious teaching forecast the discoveries and scientific methods of our day. This was because they had grasped universal principles.

Since the memorable evening in July, 1858, in which the views of Darwin and Wallace on the principles of variation and selection in the natural world were sent to the Linnaean Society in London, the leading scientists have laid great stress upon the doctrine of the survival of the "fittest" as the true explanation of progress in the natural world. It was apparently made clear by Darwin, and supported by sufficient evidence, that "any being, if it vary however slightly, in any manner profitable to itself, under the complex and somewhat varying conditions of life, will have a better chance of surviving, and thus be naturally selected."

This principle, since that day, has been thoroughly worked out in practically all the important fields of both the plant and animal world. Moreover, the doctrine of evolution, dependent upon this principle, has exerted so great an influence upon the process of investigation and thinking in all fields of activity that the resulting change in method has amounted to a revolution. The principle is applied not only in the field of biology, but also in the realm of astronomy, where we study the evolution of worlds, and in psychology, history, social science, where we speak of the development of human traits and of the growth of economic, political and social institutions.

It is necessary to remember in applying such a brief statement of a principle, that the words are used in a highly technical sense. The word "fittest" by no means need imply the best from the point of view of beauty or strength or usefulness in nature; nor does it necessarily mean, in reference to society, best from the point of view of morals or a higher civilization. Rather the "fittest" means the being best adapted to the conditions under which it is living, or to its environment. As a matter of fact, it is the general opinion that in practically all fields this principle works toward progress in the highest and best sense; but it is always a matter for specific study as well as of great scientific interest and importance, to determine where and how the variation and the corresponding selection tend to promote the morally good. Especially is this true in the study of society, where we should endeavor to see whether or not the "fittest" means also the highest from the moral and religious point of view.

The story of the flood gives us a most interesting example of the way in which the ancient Hebrews looked upon such a process of selection in the moral and religious world and taught it as a divine principle. It is, therefore, one of the most suggestive and interesting of the writings of the early Israelites.

VI.

THE SURVIVAL OF THE FITTEST IN SOCIAL AND POLITICAL LIFE.

From our modern point of view, the ancient Hebrew writers had a far deeper knowledge of moral and religious questions than of natural science. They had a far keener sense of what was socially beneficial than of what was scientifically true. However we may estimate their knowledge of geology and biology, we must grant that their beliefs regarding the good and ill effects of human action have in them much that is universally true, even though we may not follow them throughout in their theories of divine wrath and immediate earthly punishment of the wicked.

But is it not true almost invariably, if we look at social questions of every kind in a comprehensive way, that the survival of the fittest means the survival of the morally best? That the religion which endures is of the highest type? Business success in the long run, is so strongly based upon mutual confidence and trust, that, especially in these later days of credit organization, the dishonest man or even the tricky man cannot prosper long. A sales manager of a prominent institution said lately that the chief difficulty that he had with his men was to make them always tell the truth. For the sake of making an important sale they were often inclined to misrepresent his goods. "But nothing," he added, "will so surely kill all business as misrepresentation." Even a gambling book-maker on the race tracks in New York, before such work was forbidden by law, is said to have proudly claimed that absolute justice and honesty toward his customers was essential to his success and had therefore become the rule of his life. Although it is sometimes said that the man who guides his life by the maxim, "Honesty is the best policy," is in reality not honest at heart, it must nevertheless be granted that in business the survival of the fittest means the survival of the most honest business man.

It may perhaps have been true in the days of Machiavelli that cruelty and treachery would aid the unscrupulous petty despot of Italy to secure and at times to maintain his dukedom; but certainly in modern days, when in all civilized countries permanently prosperous government is based ultimately upon the will of the people, the successful ruler can no longer be treacherous and cruel. Even among our so-called "spoils" politicians and corrupt bosses, who hold their positions by playing upon the selfishness of their followers and the ignorance and apathy of the public, there must be rigid faithfulness to promises, and, at any rate, the appearance of promoting the public welfare. Otherwise their term of power is short.

If we look back through the history of modern times, we shall find that the statesmen who rank high among the successful rulers of their countries are men of unselfish patriotism, and almost invariably men of personal uprightness and morality, and usually of deep religious feeling. Think over the names of the great men of the United States, and note their characters. Pick out the leading statesmen of the last half century in England, Germany and Italy. Do they not all stand for unselfish, patriotic purpose in their actions, and in character for individual honor and integrity?

The same is true in our social intercourse. Brilliancy of intellect, however important in many fields of activity, counts for relatively little in home and social life, if not accompanied by graciousness of manner, kindness of heart, uprightness of character. It may sometimes seem that the brilliant rascal succeeds, that the unscrupulous business man becomes rich, and that the hypocrite prospers through his hypocrisy. If all society were made up of men of these low moral types, would such cases perhaps be more often found than now? In a society of hypocrites, would the fittest for survival be the most skilful deceiver? Or, even there, would the adage, "There must be honor among thieves," hold, when it came to permanent organization? But, whatever your answer, society fortunately is not made up of hypocrites or rascals of any kind. With all the weakness of human nature found in every society, the growing success of the rule of the people throughout the world proves that fundamentally men and women are honest and true. Generally common human nature is for the right. Almost universally, if a mooted question touching morals can be put simply and squarely before the people, they will see and choose the right.

Fortunate it is for the world that the lessons taught by the early Hebrew writers regarding the survival of the moral and upright are true, and that good sense and religion both agree that in the long run, honor and virtue and righteousness not only pay the individual, but are essential to the prosperity of a nation.

Questions for Further Consideration.

Had most primitive peoples a tradition regarding the flood? How do you explain the striking points of similarity between the flood stories of peoples far removed from each other?

Is there geological evidence that the earth, during human history, has been completely inundated?

What do you mean by a calamity? Is it a mere accident, or an essential factor in the realization of the divine purpose in human history?

Are appalling calamities, like floods and earthquakes, the result of the working out of natural laws? Are they unmitigated evils?

Were the floods in China and the plagues in India, which destroyed millions of lives, seemingly essential to the welfare of the surviving inhabitants of those overpopulated lands?

What were the effects of the Chicago fire and the San Francisco earthquake upon these cities? How far was the development of the modern commission form of city government one of the direct results of the Galveston flood?

To what extent is the modern progress in sanitation due to natural calamities? What calamities?

Is a great calamity often necessary to arouse the inhabitants of a city or nation to the development of their resources and to the realisation of their highest possibilities? What illustrations can you cite?

How do changes in the environment of men affect the moral quality of their acts? How do circumstances affect the kind of act that will be successful? During the Chinese revolution of 1912 in Peking and Nanking, looting leaders of mobs and plundering soldiers when captured were promptly decapitated without trial. Was such an act right? Was it necessary? What conditions would justify such an act in the United States? Would the same act tend equally to preserve the government in both countries?

Subjects for Further Study.

(1) Flood Stories among Primitive Peoples. Worcester, *Genesis* 361-373; Hastings, *Dict. of Bible* Vol. II, 18-22; Extra Vol. 181-182; *Encyc. Brit.*
(2) The Scientific Basis of the Biblical Account of the Flood. Ryle, *Early Narratives of Gen.* 112-113; Davis, *Gen. and Semitic Traditions* 130-131; Driver, *Genesis* 82-83, 99; Sollas, *Age of the Earth*, 316 ff.
(3) Compare the treatment accorded their rivals and competitors for power in their various fields by the following persons: Solomon, Caesar Borgia, the late Empress Dowager of China (Tz'u-hsi), Bismarck, the great political leaders of today in Great Britain and the United States and the modern combinations of capital known as trusts.

I Kings 1; Machiavelli, *The Prince*; Douglas, *Europe and the Far East*, Ch. 17.

Did these different methods under the special circumstances result in the survival of the fittest? The fittest morally?

STUDY V

THE PIONEER'S INFLUENCE UPON A NATION'S IDEALS.

ABRAHAM, THE TRADITIONAL FATHER OF HIS RACE.—Gen. 12:1-8; 13:1-13; 16; 18, 19; 21:7; 22:1-19.

Parallel Readings.

Hist. Bible I, 73-94.
Prin of Pol., 160-175.

Jehovah said to Abraham, Go forth from thy country, and from thy kindred, and from thy father's house, to the land that I will show thee, that I may make of thee a great nation; and I will surely bless thee, and make thy name great, so that thou shalt be a blessing, I will also bless them that bless thee, and him that curseth thee will I curse, so that all the families of the earth shall ask for themselves a blessing like thine own. So Abraham went forth, as Jehovah had commanded him.—Gen. 12:1-4. *(Hist. Bible.)*

By faith Abraham when he was called, obeyed to go out into a place which he was to receive for an inheritance; and he went out not knowing whither he went. By faith he became a sojourner in the land of promise as in a land not his own, dwelling in tents, with Isaac and Jacob, the heirs with him of the same promise; for he looked for the city which hath foundations, whose builder and maker is God.—*Heb.* 11:8-10.

He that findeth his life shall lose it; and he that loseth his life for my sake shall find it—*Matt.* 10:39.

I.

THE PROPHETIC STORIES ABOUT ABRAHAM.

Many Biblical scholars claim that the data point to variant versions of the different stories about Abraham. Thus, for example, there are two accounts of his deceptions regarding Sarah, one in 12:9-13:1, and the other in 20:1-17. The oldest version of the story they believe is found in 26:1-14 and is told not of Abraham but of Isaac, whose character it fits far more consistently. Similarly there are three accounts of the covenant with Abimelech (Gen. 21:22-31, 21:25-34, and 26:15-33). The two accounts of the expulsion of Hagar and the birth of Ishmael, in Genesis 16:1-16 and 21:1-20 differ rather widely in details. In one account Hagar is expelled and Ishmael is born after the birth of Isaac, and in the other before that event. Do these variant versions indicate that they were drawn from different groups of narratives? The differences in detail are in general closely parallel to those which the New Testament student finds in the different accounts of the same events or teachings in the life of Jesus. They suggest to many that the author of the book of Genesis was eager to preserve each and every story regarding Abraham. Instead, however, of preserving intact the different groups of stories, as in the case of the Gospels, they have been combined with great skill. Sometimes, as in the case of the expulsion of Hagar, the two versions are introduced at different points in the life of the patriarch. More commonly the two or more versions are closely interwoven, giving a composite narrative that closely resembles Tatian's Diatessaron which was one continuous narrative of the life and teachings of Jesus, based on quotations from each of the four Gospels. Fortunately, if this theory is right, the group of stories most fully quoted and therefore best preserved is the early Judean prophetic narratives. When these are separated from the later parallels they give a marvelously complete and consistent portrait of Abraham.

II.

THE MEANING OF THE EARLY
PROPHETIC STORIES ABOUT ABRAHAM.

Read the prophetic stories regarding Abraham *(Hist. Bible* I, 73, 74, 79-81, 84-87, 90-92). Are these stories to be regarded simply as chapters from the biography of the early ancestor of the Hebrews or, like the story of the Garden of Eden, do they have a deeper, a more universal moral and religious significance? Back of the story of Abraham's call and settlement in Canaan clearly lies the historic fact that the ancestors of the Hebrews as nomads migrated from the land of Aram to seek for themselves and their descendants a permanent home in the land of Canaan. Abraham, whose name in Hebrew means, "Exalted Father," or as it was later interpreted, "Father of a Multitude," naturally represents this historic movement, but the story of his call and settlement in Canaan has a larger meaning and value. It simply and vividly illustrates the eternal truths that (1) God guides those who will be guided. (2) He reveals himself alone to those who seek a revelation. (3) His revelations come along the path of duty and are confined to no place or land. (4) For those who will be led by him God has in store a noble destiny. (5) Blessed are the peacemakers for they shall be called the children of God. (6) Blessed are the meek for they shall inherit the earth. Thus this marvelous story presents certain of the noblest fruits of Israel's spiritual experiences. Incidentally it also deals with the relationship between the Hebrews and their neighbors, the Moabites, across the Jordan and the Dead Sea, for Lot in these earlier stories stands as the traditional ancestor of the Moabites and Ammonites. It is evident that, like the opening narratives of Genesis, this story aimed to explain existing conditions, as well as to illustrate the deeper truths of life.

Similarly the story of the expulsion of Hagar, it is thought, aims primarily to explain the origin of Israel's foes, the nomadic Ishmaelites, who lived south of Canaan. In the inscriptions of the Assyrian king Sennacherib, Hargaranu is the name of an Aramean tribe. A tribe bearing a similar name is also mentioned in the south Arabian inscriptions. The Hagar of the story is a typical daughter of the desert. When she became the mother of a child, the highest honor that could come to a Semitic woman, she could not resist the temptation to taunt Sarah. In keeping with early Semitic customs Sarah had full authority to demand the expulsion of Hagar, for in the eye of the law the slave wife was her property. The tradition of the revelation to Hagar also represented the popular explanation of the sanctity of the famous desert shrine Beer-lahal-roi. Like most of the prophetic stories, this narrative teaches deeper moral lessons. Chief among these is the broad truth that the sphere of God's care and blessing was by no means limited to Israel. To the outcast and needy he ever comes with his message of counsel and promise. Was Abraham right or wrong in yielding to Sarah's wish? Was Sarah right or wrong in her attitude toward Hagar? Was Hagar's triumphal attitude toward Sarah natural? Was it right?

In the story of the destruction of Sodom Lot appears as the central figure. His choice of the fertile plain of the Jordan had brought him into close contact with its inhabitants, the Canaanites. Abandoning his nomadic life, he had become a citizen, of the corrupt city of Sodom. When at last Jehovah had determined to destroy the city because of its wickedness, Abraham persistently interceded that it be spared. Its wickedness proved, however, too great for pardon. Lot, who, true to his nomad training, hospitably received the divine messengers, was finally persuaded to flee from the city and thus escaped the overwhelming destruction that felt upon it. What was the possible origin of this story? *(Hist. Bible* I, 87.) What are the important religious teachings of this story? Were great calamities in the past usually the result of wickedness? Are they to-day? Do people so interpret the destruction of San Francisco and Messina? The great epidemic of cholera in Hamburg in 1892 was clearly the result of a gross neglect of sanitary precautions in regard to the water supply. At that date the cholera germ had not been clearly identified and there was some doubt regarding the means by which the disease was spread. Was sanitary neglect then as much of a sin as it would be now? May we properly say that the pestilence was a calamity visited on that city as a punishment for its sin of neglect?

Why did the prophets preserve the story of the sacrifices of Isaac? Compare the parallel teaching in Micah 6:6-8.

> With what shall I come before Jehovah,
> Bow myself before the God on high?
> Shall I come before him with burnt-offerings,
> With calves a year old?
> Will Jehovah be pleased with thousands of rams,
> With myriads of streams of oil?
> Shall I give him my first-born for my guilt,
> The fruit of my body for the sin of my soul?

Which is the most important teaching of the story: the importance of an unquestioning faith and obedience, or the needlessness of human sacrifice? Does God ever command any person to do anything that the person thinks wrong?

III.

THE PROPHETIC PORTRAIT OF ABRAHAM.

In the so-called later priestly stories regarding Abraham (see especially Gen. 17) he is portrayed as a devoted servant of the law, chiefly intent upon observing the simple ceremonial institutions revealed to him in that primitive age. With him the later priests associated the origin of the distinctive rite of circumcision. In Genesis 14 Abraham is pictured as a valiant warrior who espoused the cause of the weak and won a great victory over the united armies of the Eastern kings. Like a knight of olden times, he restored the captured spoil to the city that had been robbed and gave a liberal portion, to the priest king Melchizedek, who appears to have been regarded in later Jewish tradition as the forerunner of the Jerusalem priesthood. In the still later Jewish traditions, of which many have been preserved, he is pictured sometimes as an invincible warrior, before whom even the great city of Damascus fell, sometimes as an ardent foe of idolatry, the incarnation of the spirit of later Judaism, or else he is thought of as having been borne to heaven on a fiery chariot, where he receives to his bosom the faithful of his race. Thus each succeeding generation or group of writers made Abraham, as the traditional father of their race, the embodiment of their highest ideals.

The Abraham of the early prophetic narratives, however, is a remarkably consistent character. He exemplifies that which is noblest in Israel's early ideals. How is Abraham's faith illustrated in the prophetic stories considered in the preceding paragraph? His unselfishness and generosity? His courtly hospitality? Was his politeness to strangers simply due to his training and the traditions of the desert or was it the expression of his natural impulses? Was Abraham's devoted interest in the future of his descendants a noble quality? How are his devotion and obedience to God illustrated? In the light of this study describe the Abraham of the prophetic narratives. Is it a perfect character that is thus portrayed? Is it the product of a primitive state of society or of a high civilization?

IV.

THE TENDENCY TO IDEALIZE NATIONAL HEROES.

Is Shakespeare right in his statement that "The evil that men do lives after them; the good is oft interred with their bones"? Why do men as a rule idealize the dead? Does the primitive tendency to ancestor worship in part explain this? Is the tendency to idealize the men of the past beneficial in its effect upon the race? What would be the effect if all the iniquity of the past were remembered? The tendency to idealize national heroes is by no means confined to the Hebrews. Greek, Roman and English history abounds in illustrations. Cite some of the more striking. Why are they often thought of as descendants of the gods? Compare the popular conception of the first president of the United States and his character as portrayed in Ford's "The Real George Washington." The portraits of national heroes, even though they are idealized, exert a powerful and wholesome influence upon the nations who honor their memory. The noblest ideals in each succeeding generation are often thus concretely embodied in the character of some national hero. Compare the great heroes of Greek mythology with the early heroes of the Old Testament. Do these differences correspond to the distinctive characteristics of the Greeks and the Hebrews? Are these differences due to the peculiar genius of each race or in part to the influence exerted by the ideals thus concretely presented upon each succeeding generation? Is it probable that in the character of Abraham the traditional father of the Hebrew race was idealized? Is it possible that teachers of Israel, consciously or unconsciously, fostered this tendency that they might in this concrete and effective way impress their great teachings upon their race? If so, does it decrease or enhance the value and authority of these stories?

V.

THE REASONS FOB MIGRATION.

In the early history of most countries there comes a pressure of population upon the productive powers of the land. As numbers increase in the hunting stage game becomes scarce and more hunting grounds are needed. Tribes migrate from season to season, as did the American Indians, and eventually some members of the tribe are likely to go forth to seek new homes. Later in the pastoral stage of society, as the wealth of flocks and herds increases, more pasturage is needed and similar results follow. Even after agriculture is well established and commerce is well begun, as in Ancient Greece, colonies have a like origin. In the England of the nineteenth century Malthus and his followers taught the tendency of population to outgrow the means of subsistence—a tendency overcome only by restraints on the growth of population, or by new inventions that enable new sources of supply to be secured or that render the old ones more efficient. Emigration and pioneering are thus a normal outgrowth of a progressive growing people in any stage of civilization. What does the statement about Abraham's wealth in cattle and silver and gold show regarding the country from which he came and the probable cause of God's direction for his removal?

Immigrants and pioneers are usually the self-reliant and courageous, who dare to endure hardships and incur risks to secure for their country and posterity the benefits of new lands and broader opportunity. The trials of new and untried experiences and often of dire peril strengthen the character already strong, so that the pioneers in all lands and ages have been heroes whose exploits recounted in song and story have stirred the hearts and molded the faith of their descendants through many generations. In the light of later history what was the profound religious significance to his race and to the world, of the migration represented by Abraham? The Biblical narrative does not state the exact way in which Jehovah spoke to Abraham. Is it possible and probable that God spoke to men in that early day as he speaks to them now, through their experiences and inner consciousness? In what sense was Abraham a pioneer?

Was it for Abraham's material interest to migrate to Canaan?

VI.

THE PERMANENT VALUE AND INFLUENCE OF THE ABRAHAM NARRATIVES.

Scholars will probably never absolutely agree regarding many problems connected with Abraham. Some have gone so far as to question whether he was an historical character or not. Is the question of fundamental importance? Other writers declare it probable that a tribal sheik by the name of Abraham led one of the many nomad tribes that somewhere about the middle of the second millenium B.C. moved westward into the territory of Palestine. It is probable that popular tradition has preserved certain facts regarding his life and character. It is equally clear that the different groups of Israel's teachers have each interpreted his character and work in keeping with their distinctive ideals. Each individual narrative has an independent unity and the connection between the different accounts is far from close. Some of them aim to explain the derivation of popular names, as for example, Abraham, Isaac, and Ishmael, the sanctity of certain sacred places, as for example, Beersheba, the origin of important institutions, as for example, circumcision and the substitution of animal for human sacrifice, and the explanation of striking physical phenomena, as for example the desolate shores of the Dead Sea.

Some of these accounts, like the table of nations in Genesis 10, preserve the memory of the relationship between Israel and its neighbors. They preserve also the characteristic popular record of the early migrations which brought these peoples to Palestine, where they crystalized into the different nations that figure in the drama of Israel's history. The permanent and universal value of these stories lies, however, in the great moral principles which they vividly and effectively illustrate. The prophetic portrait of Abraham was an inspiring example to hold up before a race. The characteristics of Abraham can be traced in the ideals and character of the Israelites. They were unquestionably an important force in developing the prophet nation. He was, therefore, pre-eminently a spiritual pioneer. How far do these stories, and especially the accounts of the covenant between Jehovah and Abraham, embody the national and spiritual aspirations of the race? Are the Abraham stories of practical inspiration to the present generation? What qualities in his character are essential to the all-around man of any age? How far would the Abraham of the prophetic stories succeed, were he living in America to-day? Would he be appreciated by a majority of our citizens? Are spiritual pioneers of the type of Abraham absolutely needed in every nation and generation if the human race is to progress?

Questions for Further Consideration.

Are God's purposes often contrary to man's desires? Ever to man's best interests?

What qualities must every true pioneer possess?

What is the ultimate basis of all true politeness?

Who are some of the great pioneers of early American history? What were their chief contributions to their nation?

Is your own conscientious conception of your duty to be considered as God's command to you? Does he give any other command?

Does a high stage of civilization ennoble character or tend to degrade it?

Subjects for Further Study.

(1) Abraham in Late Jewish Tradition. Hastings, *Dict. Bib.* I, 16, 17, Ginsberg, *The Legends of the Jews*, I, pp. 185-308.
(2) The Geological History of the Dead Sea Valley. Hastings, *Dict. Bib.* I, 575-7; *Encyc. Bib.* I, 1042-6; Kent, *Bib. Geog. and Hist.*, 45-54; Smith, *Hist. Geography*, 499-516.

(3) The Original Meaning of Sacrifice. *St. O. T.*, IV, 238; Hastings, *Dict. Bib.* IV, 329-31; *Encyc. Bib.* IV, 4216-26; Smith, *Relig. of the Semites*, 213-43, 252-440; Gordon, *Early Traditions of Genesis*, 212-16.

(4) A Comparison of the Motives that Inspired the Migrations of the Ancestors of the Hebrews and our Pilgrim Fathers. Cheyney, *European Background of American History*; Andrews, *Colonial Self-Government*.

STUDY VI

THE POWER OF AMBITION.

JACOB, THE PERSISTENT.—
Gen. 28, 10-33, 20.

Parallel Readings.

Hist. Bible I, 101-21.
Hastings, Dict. Bible II, 526-535.
Prin. of Politics Ch. II.

Now as the boys grew Esau became a skilful hunter, but Jacob was a quiet man, a dweller in tents. And Isaac loved Esau—for he had a taste for game—and Rebekah loved Jacob.

Once when Jacob was preparing a stew, Esau came in from the field, and he was faint; therefore Esau said to Jacob, Let me eat quickly, I pray, some of that red food, for I am faint. (Therefore his name was called Edom, Red.) But Jacob said, Sell me first of all your birthright. And Esau replied, Alas! I am nearly dead, therefore of what use is this birthright to me? And Jacob said, Swear to me first; so he swore to him, and sold his birthright to Jacob. Then Jacob gave Esau bread and stewed lentils, and when he had eaten and drank, he rose up and went his way. Thus Esau despised his birthright.—*Hist. Bible.*

Charles Darwin when asked for the secret of his success said, "It's dogged as does it."

> Oh well for him whose will is strong!
> He suffers, but he will not suffer long;
> He suffers, but he cannot suffer wrong:
> For him nor moves the loud world's random mock,
> Nor all Calamity's hugest waves confound,
> Who seems a promontory of rock,
> That, compasst round with turbulent sound
> In middle ocean meets the surging shock,
> Tempest-buffetted but citadel-crowned.
> —Tennyson.

Life is comic or pitiful, as soon as the high ends of being fade out of sight and man becomes near-sighted and can only attend to what addresses the senses—*Emerson.*

> Who rises every time he falls
> Will sometime rise to stay.

I.

THE TWO BROTHERS, JACOB AND ESAU.

South of the Dead Sea, bounded by the rocky desert on the east and the hot barren Arabah on the west, extends the wild picturesque range of Mount Seir. It is a land of lofty heights and deep, almost inaccessible valleys, the home of the hunter and the nomad. From a few copious springs there issue clear, refreshing brooks, which run rippling through the deep ravines, but soon lose themselves in their hot, gravelly beds. A few miles further on they emerge and again disappear, as they approach the borders of the hot, thirsty wilderness that surrounds Mount Seir on every side. Here in early times lived the Edomites, a nomadic people who established themselves in this borderland of Palestine long before the Hebrews gained a permanent foothold in the land of Canaan. The name, Edom, is found in an inscription of a king of the eighth Egyptian Dynasty,

In the Biblical narrative, Esau evidently is the traditional ancestor of the Edomites, even as Jacob figures as the father of the twelve tribes. One of the aims of these narratives, it seems to many scholars, is to explain why the Israelites, the younger people, who settled latest in Palestine, ultimately possessed the land and conquered the Edomites.

The portraits of Esau and Jacob are remarkably true to the characteristics of these two rival nations. They are also faithful to human nature as we find it to-day. Of these two brothers which, on the whole, is the more attractive? Which resembles his father and which his mother? (Read the accounts of their lives, Gen. 24-27.) What noble virtues does Esau possess? What was his great fault? Reckless men or drifters with generous impulses but with no definite purpose, of whom gypsies and hoboes are extreme types, are found in every age and society. Why is it that men of the type of Esau so often in time become criminals?

II.

THE MAN WITH A WRONG AMBITION.

The modern tendency to idealize the character of Jacob, simply because he was one of the famous patriarchs, is both unfortunate and misleading. Although he vividly typifies certain characteristics of his race, the Jacob of these early prophetic accounts is portrayed with absolute fidelity and realism. His faults are revealed even more clearly than his virtues. The dominant motive in his life is ambition, but it is a thoroughly selfish ambition. In the light of the stories, state in your own words what was the exact nature of Jacob's ambition. How did it differ from that of Abraham? What methods did he use to achieve his ambition? Were these methods justifiable? What is your view of the statement, "The end justifies the means"? Try to define exactly the method of determining justifiable means. May Jacob's action be excused because he was acting under the direction of his mother?

Does a man with a selfish ambition always injure others? Does he in the end injure himself most of all? How? Every type of selfishness is directly opposed to a man's highest self-interest. Jesus continually had this large truth in mind when he declared, "He that findeth his life shall lose it, but he that loseth his life for my sake shall find it." Jesus himself illustrated this principle.

Cite other illustrations from history. From your own observation or experience.

Was Jacob, even with his wrong ambition, a stronger and more promising character than his brother Esau? Why?

Would you rather have your son a boy of strong character with vicious tendency or a weakling with harmless, virtuous inclinations?

III.

JACOB'S TRAINING IN THE SCHOOL OF EXPERIENCE.

Jacob's experiences as a fugitive well illustrate the homely proverb, "The way of the transgressor is hard." He who deceived and cheated his brother soon became the victim of deception and fraud. Most painful of all was the ever-haunting sense of fear because of the consequences of his wrong acts that followed him even in his life as an exile and, like a spectre, confronted him as he returned again to the scenes of his boyhood. These painful experiences were probably essential to the development of Jacob's character. Are there any other ways in which men of this type can be led to appreciate that their ambitions are wrong? Was Laban any more unjust or tricky in his dealing with Jacob than Jacob had been with Esau, or than Jacob was with Laban? Note the grim humor running through these stories. They are the type of stories that would be especially appreciated when told by shepherds beside the camp fire.

The most significant point in these stories is that they declare that Jehovah's care and guidance followed the selfish deceiver even as he fled the consequences of his own misdeeds. Why should that divine care shield him from the consequences of his misdeeds? Do we find such instances to-day? How do you explain them? What is the meaning of the story of Jacob's vision at Bethel? What promising elements did Jehovah find in Jacob's character? What practical lessons did Jacob learn during his sojourn in Aram?

Was Jacob really a hypocrite, or did he in fact fail to see any inconsistency between, his trickery and meanness and his worship of Jehovah? A man may be sincere in his religious worship on

Sunday and yet cheat a neighbor on Monday. Analyze carefully the nature of his religion.

IV.

THE INVINCIBLE POWER OF AMBITION AND PERSEVERANCE.

History and modern life abound in illustrations of what can be accomplished by the combination of ambition and perseverance. Cyrus, the king of a little upland province, through a remarkable series of victories became the undisputed master of south-western Asia and laid the foundations of the great Persian Empire. Julius Caesar, who transformed Rome from a republic into an empire, and Napoleon the Corsican, are the classic illustrations of the power of great ambition and dauntless persistency. Far nobler is that quiet, courageous perseverance which led Livingston through the trackless swamps and forests of Africa and blazed the way for the conquest of the dark continent. Equally significant is that noble ambition, coupled with heroic perseverance, that has enabled settlement workers to bring light to the darkest parts of our great cities.

Ambition without persistency is but a dream or hope. Observe Jacob's persistency in the Biblical stories. Does persistency, which has always been a marked characteristic of the Hebrew race, largely explain the achievements of the Jews throughout the world? Note the apparently scientific knowledge regarding breeding of lambs by Jacob in his dealings with Laban. Is it a fact recognized by science to-day? If he knew this and Laban did not, can you justify his acts? Can you justify the act of the director of a corporation who uses his prior knowledge of the business of his corporation to make profit from buying or selling its stocks? Who loses? Is he a trustee for their interests?

What is the meaning of the strange story of Jacob's midnight struggle with the angel? *(Hist. Bible* I, 119-20.) What lessons did Jacob learn from this struggle? Would you call Jacob a truly religious man, according to his light and training, or were his religious professions only hypocritical? May he have been sincere, but have had a wrong conception of religion? What is hypocrisy? Did Jacob's faith in

Jehovah, in the end prove the strongest force in his life? Is there any trace in his later years, of the selfish ambition which earlier dominated him? What are his chief interests in the latter part of his life? Did he become the strong and noble character that he might have been had he from the first been guided by a worthy ambition? Were the misfortunes that came to him in his old age due largely to his own faults reappearing in the characters of his sons?

V.

THE DIFFERENT TYPES OF AMBITION.

In the ultimate analysis it is the man's motive which determines his character as well as his acts.

"As he thinketh within himself, so is he."—Prov. 23:7.

"Man looketh on the outward appearance, but Jehovah on the heart."—I Sam. 16:7.

With many men the strongest motive is the desire to surpass others. It not only leads them to perform certain acts, but in so doing shapes their habits; and character is largely the result of man's habitual way of acting. Jacob grew up narrow and crafty because of the selfish, dwarfing nature of his ambition, At first his ambition was of a low type, that of the child which desires to acquire possessions and power simply for himself. In the child this impulse is perfectly natural. In the normally developed individual, during the years of early adolescence (the years of 14 to 16) the social and altruistic impulses begin to develop and to take the place of those which are purely egoistic or selfish. When the fully developed man fails, as did Jacob, to leave behind childish things and retains the ambitions and impulses of the child, his condition is pitiable.

Men of this type of ambition often achieve great things from the economic or political point of view. Economically they are of greater value to society than the drifter. Sometimes, however, they bring ruin and disaster to society, as well as to themselves. Despots like Herod the Great and Napoleon, corrupt political bosses, who play into the hands of certain classes at the expense of the general public, and men who employ grafting methods in business or politics, belong to this class.

VI.

THE DEVELOPMENT OF RIGHT AMBITIONS.

The desire to spare one's energies is natural to man. To gain wealth with the least expenditure of energy is said to be the chief economic motive. Most men are by nature lazy. This law of inertia applies not only in the physical world, but also in the intellectual, moral and spiritual fields. The great majority of men follow the line of least resistance. In politics and morals they accept the standards of their associates. Unconsciously they join the great army of the drifters, or followers, who preserve the traditions of the past, but contribute little to the future progress of the race. To deliver man from the control of his natural inertia he must be touched by some strong compelling power. Ambition is one great force that enables most men to overcome this inertia. The influences, therefore, which kindle ambition are among the most important which enter the life of man.

In the Orient the mother stands in especially close relation to the son. How far was Jacob's desire to surpass his brother inspired by his mother? Many of the world's greatest leaders trace the impulse which has led them to achieve directly to their parents and especially to their mothers. The mother of Charles and John Wesley is but one of the many mothers to whom the human race owes an inestimable debt. Of all the heritages which parents can leave their children none is greater than a worthy ambition. Sometimes it is the personality of a great teacher which inspires the youthful ambition and directs it in lines of worthy achievement. How much of England's greatness may be traced to the quiet influence of Arnold of Rugby! Consider the unparalleled influence of Socrates, Plato, Aristotle—all primarily teachers.

The true pastor with the spirit of a prophet is often able to guide those with whom he comes into intimate contact to great fields of service. In encouraging Sophia Smith to found Smith College that quiet New England pastor, the Reverend John M. Greene, won a high place among those in America who first appreciated the importance of education of woman. Equally great opportunities may lie before every pastor and teacher and citizen. Frequently it is the contact through literature or in life with men or women who have done heroic deeds or have won success in the face of great obstacles that kindles the youthful ambition and stirs the latent motives which in turn develop strong and noble characters. Therein lies the perennial value of the Biblical narratives.

For many men that which arouses their ambitions is the call of a great opportunity or responsibility. Note the change in General Grant's life with the outbreak of the Civil War. The unambitious tanner becomes the untiring, rigid, unconquerable soldier. Striking illustrations of this fact are many men, whose character, as well as conduct after they have been called to positions of political or judicial trust, is in marked contrast to their previous record. A corrupt lawyer has sometimes become an upright judge. The pride of office, the traditions of the bench have sustained him. It is the privilege and duty of each man, by thoughtful deliberation and study to shape and develop his own individual ambitions that they may conform to the highest ideals and thus guide him to the noblest and most worthy achievement. Of what value to a man is biography in forming his ambitions? Mention some biographies that you consider of the greatest help. In what ways are the life and teachings of Jesus of practical service in developing the ambitions of a man to-day?

Questions for Further Consideration.

Is it possible for a man without ambition to develop or to achieve anything really significant?

In your judgment, what percentage of the men in your community really think out and carefully plan their lives? What proportion drift or take the way shown them by others?

Some people consider mental or moral inertia the chief force that sustains the corrupt political boss. Is this true?

What proportion of the voters in your voting district actually study and appreciate the issues in each election?

What proportion of church members drift into their church membership, and what proportion join only after a careful study of the relative merits of the different churches?

What are the chief ambitions that stir men to action?

What was Jesus' ambition? Paul's? Florence Nightingale's? Abraham Lincoln's? Peter Cooper's? Garibaldi's? Dwight L. Moody's? Was there a common element in the ambition of each of these leaders of men?

Is the realization of the ambition to serve one's fellow-men limited to those who possess unique powers or opportunities?

Subjects for Further Study.

(1) The Law of Inheritance among the Early Semites. Hastings, *Dict. Bib.* II, 470-473; Kent, *Student's O. T.*, III; Johns, *Bab. and Assyr. Laws, Contracts and Letters*, 161-167.

(2) The Arameans. Hastings, *Dict. Bible* I, 138-139; *Encyc. Bib.* I, 276-280; Peters, *Early Heb. Story*, 45-47, 115-116; 133-134; Maspero, *Struggle of the Nations*, 126.

(3) The Psychological Connection between Ambition, Habits, Character and Public Life. *Prin. of Politics* Ch. II and III. James, *Talks to Teachers* Ch. II.

STUDY VII

A SUCCESSFUL MAN OF AFFAIRS.

JOSEPH'S ACHIEVEMENTS.—
Gen. 37, 39-48, 50.

Parallel Readings.

Hist. Bible, I, 121-150.
Hastings' Dict. Bible, II, 770-772.
Emerson, Essay on Character.

Now Israel loved Joseph more than all his other children, because he was the son of his old age; and he had made him a long tunic with sleeves. And when his brothers saw that their father loved him more than all his other sons, they hated him, and could not speak to him.

But Jehovah was with Joseph so that he became a prosperous man, and was in the house of his master the Egyptian. When his master saw that Jehovah was with him, and that Jehovah caused everything that he did to prosper in his hands, Joseph found favor in his eyes, as he ministered to him, so that he made him overseer of his house, and all that he had he put in his charge.

And Jehovah was with Joseph and showed kindness to him, and gave him favor in the sight of the keeper of the prison, so that the keeper of the prison gave to Joseph's charge all the prisoners who were in the prison, and for whatever they did he was responsible.

And Pharaoh said to Joseph, See, I have appointed you over all the land of Egypt. And Pharaoh took off his signet ring from his finger and put it upon Joseph's finger, and clothed him in garments of fine linen, and put a gold chain about his neck, and made him ride in the second chariot which he had. Then they cried before him, Bow the knee! Thus he set him over all the land of Egypt. Pharaoh also said to Joseph, I am Pharaoh, but without your consent shall no man lift up his hand or his foot in all the land of Egypt.—*Hist. Bible.*

For what is a man profited, if he shall gain the whole world and lose his own soul?—*Matt. 16:36.*

Men at some time are masters of their fates: The fault, dear Brutus, is not in our stars, but in ourselves, that we are underlings.—*Shakespeare* (Julius Caesar, Act. I, Sc. 2, L. 139).

I find the great thing in this world is not so much where we stand as in what direction we are moving. To reach the port of Heaven we must sail sometimes with the wind, and sometimes against it; but we must sail and not drift, nor lie at anchor.—*O. W. Holmes.*

> He that respects himself is safe from others;
> He wears a coat of mail that none can pierce.

It is more important to make a life than to make a living.—*Ex-Governor Russell of Massachusetts.*

I.

THE QUALITIES ESSENTIAL TO SUCCESS.

The late Samuel L. Clemens (Mark Twain) advised a young man who desired to enter business to select the firm with which he wished to be associated, then ask that they give him work, without mentioning the subject of compensation. Having secured this opportunity to demonstrate his ability and willingness to work, recognition would come in due time. This advice received the approval of many prominent business men. It concretely illustrates the fact that the first essential of success is the willingness to serve. It also emphasizes the necessity of being ready to do the work in accordance with the employer's wishes. Ultimate success also requires knowledge and trained ability. These, however, come through apprenticeship and a faithful improvement of opportunities. The Hebrew sages, with true insight, emphasized the importance of knowledge; but they taught also that wisdom, which is not only knowledge, but the power to apply it practically in the various relations of life, was far more important.

What other qualities are essential to the highest success? Is it very important that a man should have the right moral standards? How do a man's habits affect his efficiency?

Is it only the genius who is able to attain the highest success to-day in business and professional life? Do you accept George Eliot's definition of genius as "the capacity for unlimited work"? To what extent does a man's faith in God and in his fellow men determine his ability to win success? How far are they essential to the attainment of the highest type of success?

II.

THE LIMITATIONS AND TEMPTATIONS OF JOSEPH'S EARLY LIFE.

The Hebrew sage who uttered the prayer:

> Remove far from me falsehood and lies;
> Give me neither poverty nor riches;
> Feed me with the food that is needful for me.
> —Prov. 30:8.

voiced a great economic as well as moral principle. The men who are handicapped to-day in the race for success are either those who are born in homes of extreme poverty or of extreme wealth where they are unnaturally barred or shielded from the real problems and tasks of life. Which is probably the greater handicap? To which class did Joseph belong?

In what ways did his father show his favoritism towards Joseph? The Hebrew word rendered in the older translations, "coat of many colors," means literally, "long-sleeved tunic." This garment, like those worn by wealthy Chinese when in native costume, distinguished the rich or the nobility, who were not under the necessity of engaging in manual labor.

The dreams which Joseph told to his brothers reveal his high estimate of his own importance and were probably suggested by his father's attitude toward him. They were indeed a revelation of the ambitions already stirring in the young boy's mind. But Joseph required closer contact with real life in order to transform his ambitions into actual achievements.

Joseph gave his brothers cause for hatred toward him, but their action in selling him to the Ishmaelites was by no means justifiable. Nevertheless it brought to Joseph the experiences and opportunities absolutely essential to the attainment of his ultimate success. Often what seem man's greatest misfortunes are in reality the door that opens to the new and larger opportunities. In what two ways may a man meet misfortune?

III.

THE CALL OF A GREAT OPPORTUNITY.

Egypt, with its marvelous natural resources, its peculiar climate, its irrigation, which usually guarantees good crops, and its versatile people, has always been pre-eminently the land of opportunity. Especially was this true during the reigns of the powerful despots of the eighteenth dynasty, when the relations between Egypt and Palestine were exceedingly close. Thus, for example, according to contemporary records, during the reign of the great reformer king, Amenhotep IV, several Semites rose to positions of great authority. A certain Dudu (David) was one of the most trusted officials of this king. He is addressed by one of the Egyptian governors as "My lord, my father." Another Semite named Yanhamu not only had control of the storehouses of grain in the eastern part of the Nile Delta, but also directed the Egyptian rule of Palestine. The local governors of Palestine refer to him in terms which suggest that his authority was almost equal to that of Pharaoh himself. This was perhaps the Joseph of the Biblical account.

Is there any evidence that Joseph complained because of the injustice of his brothers? By loyal attention to his duties he made himself indispensable to his Egyptian master. A great temptation came to him in the new home. What influences led him to resist this temptation? Analyze his probable motives in detail.

The great injustice which he suffered and the seeming misfortune proved in turn a new door of opportunity, but this would not have been the case had not Joseph forgotten his own personal wrongs and given himself to the service of his fellow-prisoners. Was the prosperity which generally attended Joseph a miraculous gift or the natural consequences of his courageous, helpful spirit and his skill in making the best of every situation?

In modern life as in the ancient story, the place usually seeks the man who is fitted to fill it. The ever recurring complaint of employers is the scarcity of good men, especially of men able to exercise discretion in positions of responsibility. Was it Joseph's skill in interpreting Pharaoh's dreams, or his wise counsel in suggesting methods of providing for the people during famine that gave him his position of high trust and authority? Was the policy which made Pharaoh practical owner of all the land first instituted by Joseph, or was it already in force in Egypt? *(Hist. Bible*, I, 133.) In the thought of the prophetic narrative, was Joseph's fiscal system regarded as evidence of his loyalty to his master rather than of disloyalty to the interests of the people? Was the system suited to that stage and kind of civilization? Can this be cited by Socialists to-day as a valid argument in favor of public ownership of all land? If not, why not?

Three principles, illustrated by Joseph's life, are true to all time: (1) The only successful way to forget one's own burdens is to help bear another's; (2) God makes all things work together for good to those that love him; (3) he alone who improves the small opportunities will not miss the great chances of life.

IV.

THE TEMPTATIONS OF SUCCESS.

Modern life, and especially that in America to-day, is full of illustrations of the overwhelming temptations which come to the man who has had great success. Many a man has enjoyed the confidence and respect of his associates until his abilities have won for him large wealth with which apparently comes at times a misleading sense of immunity from the ordinary moral obligations. The result has been that the sterling virtues which have enabled him to win success have been quickly undermined and his public and private acts have become the theme of the public press. Instead of being an honor he has become a disgrace to his nation.

Joseph's sudden rise to power surpassed anything told in the Arabian Nights' Tales, and yet he remained the same simple, unaffected man, more thoughtful for another's interests than for his own. The supreme test came in his contact with his brothers, who had insulted and cruelly wronged him. They were completely at his mercy and he had abundant reason for ignoring the obligations of kinship. Did Joseph hide his cup in Benjamin's sack and later hold him as a hostage in order to punish his brothers or to test their honor and fidelity? Was this action wise? Did the brothers stand the test?

No class was regarded by the Egyptians with greater scorn and contempt than the shepherds to whom they entrusted their flocks, because the task of herding sheep was regarded as too menial for an Egyptian. The public recognition of his shepherd kinsmen, therefore, revealed in Joseph the noblest and most courageous qualities.

Why is such loyalty a primary obligation? Is it to-day regarded by all thoughtful men as one of the clearest evidences of a strong character? Can you give any modern illustrations, perhaps among your acquaintances? What is a snob? Did Joseph leave undone any act which loyalty to his kinsmen could prompt? Is Joseph's character as portrayed by the prophetic account practically perfect? Of the three characters, Abraham, Jacob and Joseph, which offers more practical suggestions to the man of to-day? Which has exerted the most powerful influence upon the ideals and conduct of the human race?

V.

THE STANDARDS OF REAL SUCCESS.

It is natural and inevitable that the various social classes of each succeeding generation should define their standards of success concretely, that is, by the lives and achievements of those who have done great things. In certain social groups the world's champion prize fighter is the beau ideal of success. Among the Camorrists of Italy that ideal is the successful blackmailer. In many sections of our great cities the powerful ward boss, whatever be his methods, is regarded as the embodiment of success. Too often in America to-day, both in the public press and in the public mind, the multi-millionaire is regarded as the pre-eminently successful man. Although the power to amass wealth is evidence of marked ability, the homage paid to it is one of the most sinister tendencies in American life. Ordinarily it means that the ambitions and achievements of a Jacob, rather than those of a Joseph, are set before the youth as the supreme goal for which to strive. A most hopeful element in the present situation is that many of the world's wealthiest men are proclaiming their sense of responsibility to society in ways both practical and impressive. Far more significant than their actual gifts is this public declaration that each man is indeed his brother's keeper, and that no man has a right to use his wealth simply for his own pleasure.

Leonidas and his fearless patriotic followers at Thermopylae left an impress upon Greek life and character that did not fade for centuries. The spirit of Robert Bruce still lingers among the crags and heather-clad hills of Scotland. The patriotic devotion of Garibaldi has imparted a new character to the Italian race. Two hundred million of the world's inhabitants still bear the imprint of the fiery faith and fanaticism of Mahomet.

America is rich in its memories of the achievements of such as Washington, Lincoln, Morse, Beecher and Emerson. What characters in all history seem to you the best examples of real success? What men and women in the present generation? How can the great majority of the boys and girls and the men and women of to-day be led to accept those higher ideals of success which are the lodestones drawing on the race to higher achievement?

VI.

THE METHODS OF SUCCESS.

The story is told of the late President Garfield that in the heat of a political campaign one of his lieutenants suggested that he adopt an exceedingly questionable policy. When Mr. Garfield objected, his lieutenant replied, "No one will know it." "But I shall know," was the quick reply.

> —"To thine own self be true,
> And it must follow, as the night the day,
> Thou canst not then be false to any man."
> —Hamlet, Act I, Sc. 3.

Wealth and power are worthy goals for which to strive. One of the first duties of a political party is to capture the offices, for without them in its power it cannot carry out the principles for which it stands. The possession of wealth represents vast possibilities for service. Thousands of tragic experiments have demonstrated, however, the fallacy of the seductive doctrine that the end justifies the means. The tragedy that overshadows many of the seemingly most successful men of to-day is the memory of the iniquitous methods whereby they have acquired wealth or mounted to power. Lavish philanthropy and the beneficent use of power can never wholly blot out from the public mind or from the mind of the successful man the memory of certain questionable acts that at the time seemed essential to the realization of a great policy.

A keen, well-informed student of modern economic conditions has asserted that no man can succeed in business life today and remain true to the teachings of Jesus. Is this true? Is it true in professional life? Is it true in politics? One of our most prominent statesmen has said that he would have found it impossible to succeed and maintain his independence if he had been compelled to earn his living. He would have been compelled either to yield to the boss or quit politics. Who are some of the men in public life who are gaining success and yet maintaining Christian principles? If the ultimate ideal of real success is service, is there any other way in which men may obtain success? Is this true of every department of human effort? Does this principle make it possible for every man, however limited his ability and opportunities, to attain real success?

Questions for Further Consideration.

How would you define genius? Edison called it 2% of inspiration and 98% of perspiration. (But see James, *Talks to Teachers*.)

Is the chief difference between the successful and the unsuccessful man the ability to recognize and seize opportunities?

Would Joseph's policy in dealing with Pharaoh's subjects meet with public approval to-day?

Could Joseph have succeeded as well in a republic?

Does Joseph's land policy justify the single tax? Or serfdom such as Joseph countenanced?

What place does loyalty to humble friends and kinsmen take in the making of great and noble characters?

Would you say that the ultimate standard of all real success is service?

Would it be wise for the state to enforce service for the public good by a heavy, progressive inheritance tax?

What justification is there for such a modification of Joseph's land policy, as the single tax? (See George, *Progress and Poverty*; Seligman, *Essays on Taxation*, 64-94.)

Do you think that a man earning his own living can expect to-day to succeed in politics and maintain his self-respect as an independent thinker?

Subjects for Further Study.

(1) The Origin and Literary Form of the Joseph Narratives. Kent, *Student's O. T.* I, 126-127; Hastings, *Dict. Bible* II, 767-769; Smith, *O. T. History*, 54-55.
(2) Contemporary Parallels to the Joseph of the Biblical Narratives. Hastings' *Dict. Bible* II, 772-775.
(3) Compare and Contrast the Achievements of Joseph, Bismarck and Cecil Rhodes.

STUDY VIII

THE TRAINING OF A STATESMAN.

MOSES IN EGYPT AND THE WILDERNESS.—EX. 1:1; 7:5.

Parallel Readings.

Goodnow, F. J., Comparative Administrative Law.
Hist. Bible I, 151-69.

And he went out on the following day and saw two men of the Hebrews striving together; and he said to the one who was doing the wrong, Why do you smite your fellow-workman? But he replied, Who made you a prince and a judge over us? Do you intend to kill me as you killed the Egyptian? Then Moses was afraid and said, Surely the thing is known. When, therefore, Pharaoh heard this thing, he sought to him Moses. But Moses fled from the presence of Pharaoh and took up his abode in the land of Midian.

And Jehovah said, I have surely seen the affliction of my people that are in Egypt, and have heard their cry of anguish, because of their taskmasters, for I know their sorrows; and I am come down to deliver them out of the power of the Egyptians, and to bring them up out of that land to a land, beautiful and broad, to a land flowing with milk and honey; Go and gather the elders of Israel together and say to them, Jehovah, the God of your fathers, the God of Abraham, Isaac and Jacob, hath appeared to me, saying,

I have surely visited you, and seen that which is done to you in Egypt, and I have said I will bring you up out of the affliction of Egypt to a land flowing with milk and honey. And they shall hearken to thy voice; and thou shalt come, together with the elders of Israel, to the king of Egypt, and ye shall say to him, "Jehovah, the God of the Hebrews, hath appeared to us; and now let us go, we pray thee, three days' journey into the wilderness, that we may sacrifice to Jehovah our God."—*Hist. Bible.*

Hold on; hold fast: hold out—patience is genius.

Let us have faith that right makes might, and in that faith let us dare to do our duty as we understand it.—*Lincoln.*

I.

THE EGYPTIAN BACKGROUND OF THE BONDAGE.

The one contemporary reference to Israel thus far found in the Egyptian inscriptions comes from the reign of Merneptah the son of Ramses II. It implies that at the time at least part of the Hebrews were in the land of Palestine:

Plundered is Canaan with every evil;
Askalon is carried into captivity,
Gezer is taken;
Yenoam is annihilated,
Israel is desolated, her seed is not,
Palestine has become a widow for Egypt.
All lands are united, they are pacified.
Every one who is turbulent has been found by King Merneptah.

The testimony of the oldest Biblical narratives regarding the sojourn of the Hebrews in Egypt is, also, in perfect accord with the picture which the contemporary Egyptian inscriptions give of the period. Furthermore, the Egyptian historians never distinguished the different races in their midst, but rather designated the foreign serf class by a common name. The absence of detailed reference to the Hebrews is therefore perfectly natural. It seems probable that not all but only part of the tribes which ultimately coalesced into the Hebrew nation found their way to Egypt. The stories regarding Joseph, the traditional father of Ephraim and Manasseh, imply that these strong central tribes, possibly together with the southern tribes of Benjamin and Judah, were the chief actors in this opening scene in Israel's history.

The Biblical narratives apparently disagree regarding the duration of the sojourn in Egypt. The reference in Gen. 15:16, which, some writers think, comes from the northern Israelite group of stories, implies that it was a period of between one hundred and one hundred and fifty years. The same duration is suggested by the priestly writer in Numbers 26:57-59. The later traditions tend to extend the period. If, as seems probable, the Hebrews first found their way to Egypt during the reign of Amenhotep IV, who reigned between 1375 and 1358 B.C., the older Hebrew chronology would make Ramses II, who reigned between 1292 and 1225, the Pharaoh of the oppression. Of all the Pharaohs of this period in Egypt's history the great builder and organizer Ramses II corresponds most closely to the Biblical description. He it was who filled Egypt from one end to the other with vast temples and other buildings which could have been reared only through the services of a huge army of serfs. The excavations of the Egypt Exploration fund have identified the Biblical Pithom with certain ruins in the Wady Tumilat near the eastern terminus of the modern railroad from Cairo to the Suez Canal. This probably lay in the eastern boundary of the Biblical land of Goshen, which seems to have included the Wady Tumilat and to have extended westward to the Nile delta. Here were found several inscriptions bearing the Egyptian name of the city P-Atum, house of the god Atum. The excavations also laid bare a great square brick wall with the ruins of store chambers inside. These rectangular chambers were of various sizes and were surrounded by walls two or three yards in thickness. Contemporary inscriptions indicate that they were filled with grain from the top and were probably used for the storing of supplies to be used by the armies of Ramses II in their Asiatic campaigns. This city was founded by Ramses II, who during the first twenty years of his reign, developed and colonized the territory east of the Nile delta including the Biblical land of Goshen. A contemporary inscription also states that he founded near Pithum the house of Ramses, a city with a royal residence and temples. Thus the inferences in the first chapter of Exodus regarding the historical background are in perfect accord with the facts now known from other sources regarding the reign of Ramses II. In transforming the land of Goshen into a cultivated, agricultural region the nomadic Hebrews were naturally put to task work by the strong-handed ruler of Egypt. That the Hebrews were restive under this tyranny was natural, inevitable. Apparently their rebellious attitude also increased the burden which was placed upon them. The memory of the crushing Hyksos invasion, which meant the rule of Egypt by nomadic invaders from Asia, was still fresh in the minds of the Egyptians. They both looked down upon and feared the nomad immigrants on their eastern border. In the light of these facts it is possible to understand the motives which influenced Ramses II cruelly to oppress the Hebrews. He endeavored, by forced labor and rigorous peonage, not only to avail himself of their needed services, but also to crush their spirit and by force to hold in subjection the alarmingly large serf class which was found at this time in the land of Egypt. Was any other procedure to be expected from a despotic ruler of that land and day?

II.

THE MAKING OF A LOYAL PATRIOT.

The story of Moses' birth and early childhood is one of the most interesting chapters in Biblical history. It is full of human and dramatic interest. The great crisis in Moses' early manhood came when he woke to a realization of his kinship with the despised and oppressed serfs and an appreciation of the cruel injustice of which they were the helpless victims. Was Moses justified in resisting the Egyptian taskmaster? Are numbers essential to the rightness of a cause? What right had Ramses II to demand forced labor from the immigrants within his border? Was he justified in his method of exacting tribute? Is peonage always disastrous not only to its victims but also to the government imposing it?

Did Moses show himself a coward in fleeing from the land of Egypt? Naturally he went to the land of Midian. The wilderness to the east of Egypt had for centuries been the place of refuge for Egyptian fugitives. From about 2000 B.C. there comes the Egyptian story of Sinuhit, an Egyptian prince, who, to save his life, fled eastward past the "Wall of the Princes" which guarded the northeastern frontier of Egypt. On the borders of the wilderness he found certain Bedouin herdsmen who received him hospitably. These "sand wanderers" sent him on from tribe to tribe until he reached the land of Kedem, east of the Dead Sea, where he remained for a year and a half. Later he found his way to the court of one of the local kings in central Palestine where he married and became in time a prosperous local prince.

III.

THE SCHOOL OF THE WILDERNESS.

The story of Moses is in many ways closely parallel to that of Sinuhit. Among the Midianite tribes living to the south and southeast of Palestine he found refuge and generous hospitality. The priest of the sub-tribe of the Kenites received him into his home and gave him his daughter in marriage. Note the characteristic Oriental idea of marriage. Here Moses learned the lessons that were essential for his training as the leader and deliverer of his people.

The Kenites figure in later Hebrew history as worshippers of Jehovah and are frequently associated with the Israelites. After the capture of Jericho certain of them went up with the southern tribes to conquer southern Palestine. (Judg. 1:16.) It was Jael, the wife of Heber the Kenite (Judg. 5:24), who rendered the Hebrews a signal service by slaying Sisera, the fleeing king of the Canaanites, after the memorable battle beside the River Kishon. Many modern scholars draw the conclusion from the Biblical narrative that it was from the Kenites that Moses first learned of Yahweh (or, as the distinctive name of Israel's God was translated by later Jewish scribes, Jehovah). Furthermore it is suggested that gratitude to the new God, who delivered the Israelites from their bondage, was the reason why they proved on the whole so loyal to Jehovah. This conclusion is possible and in many ways attractive, but it is beset with serious difficulties. We know, in ancient history, of no other example of a people suddenly changing their religion. When there have been such sudden and wholesale conversions in later times they have been either under the compulsion of the sword, as in the history of Islam, or under the influence of a far higher religion, as when Christianity has been carried to heathen peoples on a low stage of civilization. Do the earliest Hebrew traditions imply that the ancestors of the Israelites were worshippers of Jehovah? Is it not probable that Moses fled to the nomadic Midianites not only because they were kinsmen but because they were also worshippers of Jehovah?

In any case Moses' life in Midian tended to intensify his faith in Jehovah. The title of his father-in-law implies that this priest ministered at some wilderness sanctuary. In the light of the subsequent Biblical narrative was this possibly at the sacred spring of Kadesh or on the top of the holy mountain Horeb (elsewhere called Sinai) where Kenites and Hebrews believed that Jehovah dwelt, or at least manifested himself? Moses, in the home of the Midian priest, was brought into direct and constant contact with the Jehovah worship. The cruel fate of his people and the painful experience in Egypt that had driven him into the wilderness prepared his mind to receive this training. His quest was for a just and strong God, able to deliver the oppressed. The wilderness with its lurking foes and the ever-present dread of hunger and thirst, deepened his sense of need and of dependence upon a power able to guide the destinies of men. The peasants of the vast Antolian plain in central Asia Minor still call every life-giving spring, "God hath given." The constant necessity of meeting the dangers of the wilderness and of defending the flocks entrusted to Moses' care developed his courage and power of leadership and action. What other great leaders of Israel were trained in this same school? What was the effect of their wilderness life upon the early New England pioneers?

IV.

MOSES' CALL TO PUBLIC SERVICE.

The solitude of the wilderness gave Moses ample opportunity for profound reflection. His previous experiences made such reflection natural, indeed inevitable. Borne by the caravans over the great highway from the land of the Nile or from desert tribe to tribe came occasional reports of the cruel injustice to which his kinsmen in Egypt were subjected. In these reports he recognized the divine call to duty. When perhaps at last the report came that the mighty despot Ramses II was dead, Moses like his later successor Isaiah (Is. 6) saw that the moment had come for decision and action.

It looks to many scholars as if three originally distinct versions of Moses' call have been welded together in the narrative of Exodus 3, 4 and 6. Each differs in regard to detail (Hist. Bible I, 161-5). According to the early Judean prophetic account Jehovah spoke audibly to Moses from the flaming thorn bush. In the Northern Israelite version the moment of decision came to him as he stood with his flock on the sacred mountain Horeb. Like Isaiah in his memorable vision of Jehovah's presence, the inner consciousness of God and the compelling sense of duty led him to cry out: "Here am I." Likewise in the late priestly story God's presence and character were so deeply impressed upon him that he seemed to bear an audible voice, according to the view of those who accept this interpretation, even though the later priests believed and taught that God was a spirit, not like man clothed in flesh and blood. Thus the different groups of Hebrew narratives in their characteristic way record the essential facts in Moses' call to public service. Each has preserved certain important elements in that call, and the late editor has done well to combine them. Even as Isaiah caught his supreme vision of Jehovah and of duty in the temple, so to Moses the prophetic call probably came on the lofty heights of the mountain in which he, in common with the Kenites, believed God dwelt. The wilderness with its flaming bush spoke to him God's message. Recent writers have felt and forcibly interpreted the fascination and the message of the desert and plain, none more vividly than the Welsh writer Rhoscomyl in describing the experience of one of his rough, self-reliant cowboy heroes:

"Two days ago he was riding back, alone, in the afternoon, from an unsuccessful search after strayed horses, and suddenly, all in the lifting of a hoof, the weird prairie had gleamed into eerie life, had dropped the veil and spoken to him; while the breeze stopped, and the sun stood still for a flash in waiting for his answer. And he, his heart in a grip of ice, the frozen flesh a-crawl with terror upon his loosened bones, white-lipped and wide-eyed with frantic fear, uttered a yell of horror as he dashed the spurs into his panic-stricken horse, in a mad endeavor to escape from the Awful Presence that filled all earth and sky from edge to edge of vision.

"Then almost in the same flash, the unearthly light died out of the dim prairie, the veil swept across into place again; and he managed to check his wild flight, and look about him. His empty lips were gibbering without a sound escaping them, and his very heart shivered with cold, for all the brassy heat of the day. But the breeze was wandering on again; under the great sun the prairie spread dim to the southwest, and tawny to the northeast; only between his own loose knees the horse trembled in every limb, and mumbled the bit with dry mouth. All was as before in earth and sky, apparently, but not in his own self. It was as if his spirit stood apart from him, putting questions which he could not answer, and demanding judgment upon problems which he dare not reason out.

"Then he remembered what this thing was which had happened. The prairie had spoken to him, as sooner or later it spoke to most men that rode it. It was a something well known amongst them, but known without words, and as by a subtle instinct, for no man who had experienced it ever spoke willingly about it afterwards. Only the man would be changed; some began to be more reckless, as if a dumb blasphemy rankled hidden in their breasts. Others, coming with greater strength perhaps to the ordeal, became quieter, looking squarely at any danger as they face it, but continuing ahead as though quietly confident that nothing happened save as the gods ordained."

The motive power in all of Moses' later work was that transforming, vivid sense of Jehovah's presence that came to him on the barren mountain peak.

Also fundamental to his call was the recognition of the crying need of his disorganized, oppressed kinsmen in Egypt. This appealed to all the instincts begotten by his shepherd training; for they were a shepherdless flock in the midst of wolves. Through the ages the inhabitants of the parched, stony wilderness had looked with hungry eyes upon the tree-clad hills and green fields of Palestine. The early traditions of his ancestors also glorified this paradise of the wilderness wanderer and led Moses to look to it as the haven of refuge to which he might lead his helpless kinsmen. Vividly and concretely the ancient narrative tells of the struggle in the mind of Moses between his own diffidence and consciousness of his limitations on the one side and on the other his sense of duty and the realization of Jehovah's power to accomplish what seemed to man miraculous. Was Moses' inner experience like that of the other great Hebrew prophets? Who? Like that of Jesus? Does every man who undertakes a great service for humanity today pass through a somewhat similar struggle? How about Grant on leaving his home at Galena, Illinois? Lincoln at the great crisis of his life?

V.

THE EDUCATION OF PUBLIC OPINION.

Like every man who catches a vision of a great need and undertakes to meet it, Moses had to educate public opinion. Whatever the form of government may be, whether monarchy or democracy, it must ultimately rest upon the will of the people, and the shaping of that will is often a statesman's task. In a democracy the expression of the people's will is readily determined at every election, although in many cases, owing to the number of issues, this result is not clearly seen.

In a despotism like Egypt there is no ready expression of a people's will. However great their sufferings, they must endure until they feel that the evils of revolt are less than the evils of oppression. Then, by means of a revolution, they carry out their will. In what ways did the Exodus resemble, in what ways differ from a revolution? Compare Moses with Washington or Samuel Adams as leader of a revolution. During the last few years in China there has been great dissatisfaction on the part of many millions of the people with the rule of the Manchu dynasty. It was, nevertheless, for many years the people's will rather to endure the evils of a corrupt government than to take the risk of war. At length, however, after years of propaganda by skilful leaders war appeared to them the lesser evil and their will was carried out by force of arms. The government, in this direct way, was forced to recognize the will of the people and to grant their requests.

A statesman considers not merely his own views regarding the best methods of governing his country or of gaining special ends, but he must carefully consider also what plans can in practice be carried out. In all free governments only those policies can be put into effect that meet the approval of the people; and one of the greatest gifts of a statesman is the ability to ascertain, with few mistakes, how far his proposed policies meet the public will and how he can so put his plans before the people as to convince them of their benefits.

In the later days of the Egyptian bondage the Israelites made frequent complaint of the oppression of the Pharaohs, bemoaning their fate as serfs, but for many years after their sufferings had become severe they had not yet been roused to a determination to throw off the yoke of the oppressor. Even when Moses first attempted to rouse them to make a struggle for freedom, he could not breathe into them his own bold spirit. What measures did Moses take to incite the Israelites to action? What measures did he take to convince Pharaoh of his duty toward the Israelites? Did he present his case truthfully? Was he justified in the measures taken?

At length, not from the acts of the Israelites, but from the plagues that afflicted the Egyptians and the insistent demand of Moses, coupled with the belief that the plagues were sent on account of divine displeasure, as a punishment for unjust oppression, the Hebrews were enabled to escape. What is the contemporary Egyptian testimony regarding the plagues? *(Hist. Bible* I, 176-7.) Do the earliest Hebrew records imply that these were miracles or natural calamities peculiar to the land of Egypt? The statesmanship of Moses led him to seize the opportune time for freeing his people from bondage. Only the influence of the religious sentiments among his people and their belief in Jehovah together with the religious awe felt by the Egyptian rulers, enabled him to take advantage of the circumstances so that he could rescue his people. In most countries religion is a powerful influence often made use of by rulers, sometimes for good, sometimes for ill, to direct the action of their subjects. The Greek church in Russia has for many decades been, perhaps, the most important weapon by which the Russian Czars have kept their people in peaceful submission. If China loses her Mongolian provinces, it will be because the religious leaders of Mongolia are controlling their people. Can you give in the United States an example of a people largely dominated by the religious motive which controls most of the affairs of their every-day life? How far was the religious motive responsible for the settlement and upbuilding of the New England Colonies? How far and in what ways may a statesman to-day appeal to the moral and religious feelings of the people in order to promote national and international welfare?

VI.

THE TRAINING OF MODERN STATESMEN.

In training administrative officers in the leading countries of Europe and in the United States, emphasis is laid upon a knowledge of history, of constitutional, administrative and international law, politics, economics, diplomacy and any other subjects that may fall within the scope of action of the special official. When, however, a law-maker or a high administrative official deals at first hand with a great population, it is extremely important that he be so experienced and so fitted by temperament that he may know his people. He must see how far he can go without arousing too much opposition. Even in promoting good measures, it is often essential not to go too fast, if he is to succeed.

Every statesman of modern times, as well as those of bygone days, must have the interests of the people genuinely at heart if he is to be, in the best sense of the word, successful. What did Moses seek for his people? Liberty? Prosperity? Religious freedom?

Confucius, the great Chinese sage, from his study of human nature and of government five centuries before Christ, had learned that the rule of justice in the state promoted prosperity. At length a young ruler made him his prime minister. The result of his wise and just measures was to bring into his country so large a number of immigrants who preferred to live in a country where justice reigned, that the prosperity aroused the envy and hostility of the neighboring states. In consequence measures were taken to put an end to this just rule, which was felt to be so detrimental to other kings, unwilling to adopt the same just means. Finally the wise Confucius was treacherously driven from his post, not, however, until he had proved that the counsels of justice and religion were those best suited to the welfare of the state. This is a common experience in all lands and ages; but perhaps nowhere else has the lesson been so frequently and so thoroughly taught as in the history of the Hebrews, that the most essential factor in a statesman's training is the acceptance of the principles of justice and righteousness. In other words—"God is the most important factor in human progress."

Questions for Further Consideration.

Is it the duty of a government, in order to promote the welfare of its people, to set aside at times the personal convenience, even the personal welfare of individuals or of certain classes? If an inheritance tax falls heavily upon the heirs of a rich man, ought the state to collect it? On what grounds is a state justified in withholding liberty from criminals? From children?

Many of our states compel citizens to work in repairing country roads. Is this temporary peonage? How do you justify a state in compelling citizens to risk their lives in war? In what circumstances would a state be justified in compelling its citizens to labor? Did circumstances justify Pharaoh? Why were he and his kingdom punished?

Is it ever right, for an individual to raise his hand against a recognized and established authority? Or, when there is an established government, should an individual ever attempt to punish crime or avenge personal wrong? Were our revolutionary forefathers right in resisting the demands of King George? Are numbers essential to the rightness of a cause?

In what ways does God to-day call men to do an important task? Do you consider Lincoln a man raised up by God for a purpose and called by him to service? If so, how did the call come? Was Moses' call similar? Should a clergyman have a definite call to his life-work? Should every man? Does every man have such a call, if he but interprets rightly his experiences?

A working girl had seen the story of Moses at a moving picture show. Afterwards she commented as follows: "Our walking delegate is a regular Moses. He said to the factory boss, 'You let my people go.'" In what respect is the labor struggle to-day similar to that in Egypt under Moses?

Subjects for Further Study.

(1) The Egyptian System of Education. Breasted, *Hist. of the Ancient Egyptians*, 92-94, 395; *Hist. of Egypt*, 98-100; Maspero, *Dawn of Civilization*, 288; Erman, *Life of the Ancient Egyptians*, 328-368.

(2) Origin of the Jehovah Religion. Budde, *Religion of Israel*, 1-38; Gordon, *Early Traditions of Gen.*, 106-110; Hastings, *Dict. of the Bible*, Extra Vol. 626-627.

(3) The Practical Training for Statesmanship of Augustus, Gladstone and Lincoln. Plutarch, *Lives of the Emperors*; Morley, *Life of Gladstone*; A. good Biographical Dictionary; Brown, *The Message of the Modern Pulpit*.

(4) Compare the government of Egypt under Pharaoh with that in China in the days of Confucius and with that of Greece in the days of the siege of Troy. Homer, *Iliad and Odyssey; Life of Confucius*.

STUDY IX

THE ORIGIN AND GROWTH OF LAW.

MOSES' WORK AS JUDGE AND PROPHET.—Ex. 18; 1-27; 33:5-11.

Parallel References.

Hist. Bible I, 198-203.
Prin. of Politics, Ch. VI.
Maine, Ancient Law.

Jehovah spake to Moses face to face, as a man speaketh unto his friend—Ex. 33: 11.

And Moses chose able men out of all Israel, and made them heads over the people, rulers of thousands, rulers of hundreds, rulers of fifties, and rulers of tens. And they judged the people at all seasons: the hard cases they brought unto Moses, but every small matter they judged themselves—Ex. 18:25, 26.

Love is the fulfilling of the law.—St. Paul.

> Now this is the Law of the Jungle—as old and as true as the sky;
> And the Wolf that shall keep it may prosper, but the Wolf that shall break it must die.
> As the creeper that girdles the tree-trunk the Law runneth forward and back—

> For the strength of the Pack is the Wolf, and the strength
>   of the Wolf is the Pack.
> Now these are the Laws of the Jungle, and many and
>   mighty are they;
> But the head and the hoof of the Law and the haunch and
>   the bump is "Obey!"
> —Kipling.

Nothing is that errs from law.—*Tennyson*.

> In vain we call old notions fudge,
> And bend conventions to our dealing,
> The Ten Commandments will not budge,
> And stealing still continues stealing.
> —Lowell.

> If chosen men could never be alone,
> In deep mid-silence, open-doored with God
> No greatness ever had been dreamed or done.

> These roots bear up Dominion: Knowledge, Will,—
> These twain are strong, but stronger yet the third,—
> Obedience,—'tis the great tap-root that still,
> Knit round the rock of Duty, is not stirred,
> Though Heaven-loosed tempests spend their utmost skill.
> —Lowell (The Washers of the Shroud).

I.

THE NEEDS THAT GIVE RISE TO LAW.

Kipling's *Law of the Jungle*, in which he lays down the principles by which the wolf pack secured united action in its hunting, names the rules that apply almost universally to peoples in the savage stage of society. According to the researches of the best anthropologists, savages live in very loosely organized groups, with no permanent ruler, no regular family law. Each separate group has its totem, its general rules with reference to the marriage relation, to hunting and fishing, to shelter and protection. Practically there are no regular laws. The rules fixed by custom deal primarily with the marriage relation and with the securing of food and shelter. They are largely negative. If a member of the group has met with a misfortune in a certain by-path or from eating certain food or in other ways, by the action of the leader of his group that path or that food becomes taboo, and from that time on it is forbidden. The rules seem generally to be largely the product of instinct or of experience, without any law making, and they are enforced almost as instinctively by the common consent of the people.

II.

THE GROWTH OF CUSTOMARY LAW.

As this loosely associated group condenses into the tribe, all the members of which regard themselves as descended from a common ancestor, the organization becomes much more definite under a patriarchal ruler. Soon through his activities these almost instinctive habits, guided by rules, assume the nature of customs that have a sanction, often of religion, practically always of enforcement through the patriarch. No better illustration of the crystallization of customs into laws can be found than that given in Exodus 18:1-27 *(Hist. Bible,* I, 198-202). Moses sat all day long as judge to decide cases for the people until his practical-minded father-in-law, Jethro, seeing the waste of time and energy of the ruler upon whom the welfare of the tribe depended, proposed a wise plan. He advised that, instead of rendering decisions regarding each individual case, Moses should formulate the principles and leave their application to minor judges appointed by himself as rulers over thousands and over hundreds and fifties and tens. In modern days the law-making body is distinct from the judicial. Is there any reason why the judge should not be the maker of the law he interprets?

Doubtless many of the customs thus formulated by Moses had come down through the preceding ages from the Babylonian and common Semitic ancestors of the Hebrews. The most striking example of the pre-Mosaic formulation of custom into law under the sanction of the deity is found in the so-called code of Hammurabi, which comes from about 1900 B.C. At the top of the stele which records these laws this enlightened king depicted himself in a bas-relief as receiving them from the sun god, Shamash. Hammurabi looked upon himself as a shepherd chosen by the gods to care for his people. It was his duty to see "that the great should not oppress the weak, to counsel the widow and orphan, to render judgment and decide the decisions of the land, and to succor the injured," in order that "by the command of Shamash, the judge supreme of heaven and earth, justice might shine in the land." Many of the principles laid down by him are also found among the laws attributed to Moses which were afterward codified in the early decalogues.

At times, though rarely among the Hebrews, we may study custom in the making, as when in a new situation a ruler renders a decision which henceforth becomes a law. Thus David, dividing the spoil after his victory over the Amalekites, established a precedent that henceforth had binding force upon his followers (I Sam. 30); but in the majority of such cases the ruler, even when be establishes new precedents, represents himself as simply interpreting ancient custom.

As society becomes more and more complex and the interests of individuals and classes in society clash, besides the judges we find legislatures making new rules in the form of law. In the earlier communities practically all law relates to the preservation of life and of the tribe. Later, as the tribe enters the pastoral state, private property is established and laws for its care are made. Still later, with the development of a higher civilization and with the individual conscience stimulating men to care for the welfare not merely of their family, but of their nation, legislation considers primarily the welfare of society. Yet, as one of our great judges has lately explained, in practically all stages of society, whenever the population becomes numerous and business is so developed that we may recognize different classes in a community, legislation has been primarily in the interests of a ruling class, often at the expense of the other classes. This principle is illustrated by certain of the later Jewish ceremonial laws that brought to the priests a large income at the expense of the people. Many laws in Europe and in the United States to-day have been made clearly in the interests of certain classes in society. Can you think of some?

III.

THE AUTHORITY UNDERLYING ALL LAW.

Back of all laws and rules, as the fundamental consideration, whether consciously expressed in laws or carried out instinctively, lies the welfare of society. Among the wolves the pack that is best disciplined by the strongest and most successful leader is the one that survives. In the earlier savage groups the rules which guided united action grew up as a result of successful experience in securing food and warding off enemies. Among them the less disciplined, the less intelligently directed groups perish.

Through his fear of the unknown, stimulated by the terrible vindications of nature's laws, when poison and pestilence and storms and floods do their deadly work, the savage feels the presence of unknown forces that he calls gods, and he thus gives to his rules of action the sanction of divinity. And as society develops through the pastoral, agricultural and industrial stages into the tribe and state, with the development of religion and the growing sense of right and of responsibility to one's fellow men, this religious sanction of the law still abides. In the earlier days the sanction was due to fear of the vengeance of the gods. In later society it is the sense of right and justice and love for one's fellow men, springing from the firm belief in the divine creation and direction of the universe and in God's care for men.

But as this sense of fear or right or justice or love, associated with a Being felt to be divine, is not universal, inasmuch as many members of society are found ready to act selfishly, taking the law into their own hands, force is needed in all stages of society to put the rules and laws into effect. With every law, as Austin says, must go a penalty. But as society grows more and more humane the sense of obligation of each individual for the welfare of his fellows grows, until in the best society laws are made and obeyed by most citizens, not from a sense of fear of punishment, but mainly out of goodwill to others. A sense of justice prevails and the sanction of law becomes not so much fear of the penalty imposed, as the moral and religious sense of the individual and of society. Why, for example, do you obey the law against stealing?

IV.

MOSES' RELATION TO THE OLD TESTAMENT LAWS.

The Hebrew laws given in the Old Testament are generally known as the laws of Moses, and the assumption of many readers in earlier years has been that the different codes were practically formulated by Moses himself. The subsequent study of the Old Testament long ago suggested to many that this view may be mistaken. The oldest records of his work and the fact that, as creator of the Hebrew nation after the Exodus and as leader and prophet be rendered important judicial decisions, have well justified the belief that he was the real founder of what is called the Mosaic Law. As stated in Exodus 18, he did actually formulate the principles by which decisions were made by the rulers whom he appointed over thousands and over hundreds, fifties and tens. He may have even put into form the principles found in the earliest decalogues. Moreover, as the Israelites in their later history were led to formulate new rules of action, they based these upon the principles of justice, religion and civil equality found in the earlier decalogues. While the specific rules of living must have changed materially, as the Israelites changed their habits of living from those of wanderers in the wilderness to those adapted to their early settlements in Canaan and afterward to the settled conditions under the monarchy, they would still base their laws upon these earlier principles. Hence it was not unnatural to ascribe the origin of these laws to Moses, nor is it to-day inaccurate to speak of them as the Mosaic code, even though they may have been put into their present form at different periods remote from one another, and by rulers, prophets and priests whose occupations and attitude toward life were widely different. Back of practically all these laws are the fundamental beliefs that the Israelites are the people chosen of God, that to him they owe allegiance and that from him they derive, in principle at least, the laws under which they live.

V.

THE DEVELOPMENT OF MODERN LAW.

Not merely the Hebrews, but practically all ancient nations ascribe the origin of their laws either to a deity or to some great ancestral hero. As already noted, the code of Hammurabi is represented as having been given to him directly by the god Shamash. In the early days of Greek history, the laws of Solon and Draco were formulated. In India we find the laws of Manu, in China the teachings of Confucius, and so on throughout all of the great nations. In some instances, doubtless, many of the laws were actually formulated under the direction of the person to whom they are ascribed; but in many others, as perhaps in the case of the Mosaic code, there was some great judge or king under whose direction certain principles were laid down and simple laws or precedents established, and as a result all later developments were ascribed to him.

In modern times, when legislative bodies are found in limited monarchies as well as in republics, the methods of legislation are necessarily different. Although chosen bodies of men come together to legislate for the benefit of society, as represented by the state, there is still a normal tendency for the ruling class to feel that it is to a great extent the state, and it does not forget its own needs. This class legislation was doubtless existent to a certain extent even when the laws, supposed to be of divine origin, were formulated by prophets and priests, for the real public character of the laws was dependent primarily upon the unselfish beliefs, social and religious, of the writers, whether kings or priests. No one is able to free himself entirely from the influence of class prejudice.

Like the legislatures the courts even are also the product of their times, though naturally conservative. No law can long exactly fit changing conditions. The judge must adapt a law made by one generation to the needs of the next. In so doing he bends it to suit his times, and to further the welfare of his state.

If aeroplanes carrying goods from Pennsylvania to New York over the State of New Jersey let them fall and damage the property of a resident of New Jersey, can our courts invoke the Interstate Commerce Law made before aeroplanes were invented?

And yet there has been throughout the individual history of each nation a gradual improvement in the living conditions of the masses of people, even in the tribal state. As it proved more profitable to preserve a worker than to kill him, captives in war were not slain, but enslaved. As society became more settled, the custom of personally avenging one's wrong by slaying an enemy was modified. Cities of refuge were established, where innocent victims might escape the avengers. All down through the ages there has been a growing tendency to adapt the punishment to the crime, to temper justice with mercy, to realize that the aim of all law is not vengeance or punishment, but the promotion of the best interests of society through the wise administration of justice.

VI.

THE ATTITUDE OP THE CITIZENS TOWARD THE LAW.

Among savages, as has been said, there is no formulation of law. There is the instinct of the individual to preserve his own life, and there are rules that must be followed if the people are to survive. As has been truly said: "The love of justice is simply in the majority of men the fear of suffering injustice." The instinct of preservation and sheer necessity compel the people almost unconsciously to follow the rules of their leader.

In most patriarchal societies the fear of the god of the tribe, the overpowering influence of custom and the unswerving directness of the punishment of the man who violates it tend to prevent the development of individuality and of independent thinking; and the normal attitude of practically every person is to obey the customs and the laws, although often those laws leave to the individual a range of action not found in later civilized states. But as the sense of right and justice and the desire to promote the public welfare grow, individualism grows also. Each individual, thrown upon his own resources, learns to think and question and judge. In democratic states he learns to take upon himself the responsibility for his acts, and at length the view becomes prevalent that law exists for the benefit of society. The individual, in judging himself and his attitude toward society, feels that the law must be obeyed because obedience promotes the public welfare. Even when he believes that a law is unwise, or even unjust, he hesitates to violate it, not only because he might be punished therefor, but primarily because it has become wrong, according to his conscience, to violate a law that has been adopted by the representatives of his fellow citizens as just and beneficial. Thus the individual, in later even more than in earlier times, obeys the laws not merely from selfish, but from social and religious motives.

Questions for Further Consideration.

Can you name any modern laws that you think have been framed in the interests of a special social class?

Do you think that the people of to-day are recreant in their respect for or adherence to law?

What do you consider to be the value of such institutions as those at West Point and Annapolis in their influence on the enforcement of law and discipline?

When we speak of "Government of the people, by the people, and for the people," whom exactly do we mean by "people"? Does the word have the same meaning in each of these phrases?

Is it ever right to violate a law of the land? Some people contend that an individual ought to break a human law, provided that it is contrary to divine law. What is divine law? Who decides? Shall the individual decide, or is that the duty of the community? Or of the clergy? Was it right for the Abolitionists to violate the provisions of the fugitive slave law? Were this handful of men, able and conscientious as they were, as likely to be right regarding the welfare of society as the large majority of citizens whose representatives had enacted the fugitive slave law? If a person believes our tariff laws to be unjust, is it right for him to smuggle goods?

Under what circumstances, if any, is it one's duty to disobey a law of the state? Would the fact that an individual believed it his duty to violate the law justify a judge in declining to punish him? Thoreau declined to pay a tax that he believed unjust and accepted his punishment, declaring that if he paid the penalty he might thus arouse public sentiment and secure the repeal of the law. Was John

Brown justified in attempting illegally to free slaves by force of arms?

In Great Britain the House of Lords—one of the law-making bodies—is also the highest court of appeal, although the judicial business is mostly done by law lords specially appointed for that purpose. Ought the same men to make and interpret the law? Why?

Subjects for Further Study.

(1) Origin and Growth of Hebrew Law. Hastings, *Dict. of Bible*, III, 64-67; *Ency. Bib.*, III, 2714-8; Kent, *Israel's Laws and Legal Precedents*, IV, 8-15.
(2) Growth of Primitive Law. Maine, *Ancient Law*, 109-165; Wilson, *The State*, 1-29.
(3) Judicial Decisions as a Factor in the Development of Modern Law. *Prin. of Politics*, Chap. VI, Ransom, *Majority Rule and the Judiciary*.

STUDY X

THE FOUNDATIONS OF GOOD CITIZENSHIP.

THE TEN COMMANDMENTS.—Ex. 20:1-17.

Parallel Readings.

Hist. Bible I, 194-198.
Prin. of Politics, Chap. II.
Lowell, Essay on "Democracy."

Thou shalt have no other gods before me.
Thou shalt not make unto thee a graven image.
Thou shalt not take the name of Jehovah thy God in vain.
Remember the sabbath day, to keep it holy.
Honor thy father and thy mother.
Thou shalt not kill.
Thou shalt not commit adultery.
Thou shalt not steal.
Thou shalt not bear false witness against thy neighbor.
Thou shalt not covet thy neighbor's house.—Ex. 20:3-17.

If ye know my commandments, happy are ye if ye do them.—Jesus.

Wherewithal shall I come before Jehovah, and bow myself before the High God? . . . He hath showed thee, Oh man, what is good; and what doth Jehovah require of thee but to do justly, and to love kindness, and to walk humbly with thy God?—Micah 6:6, 8.

Most religions are meant to be straight lines connecting two points—God and man. But Christianity has three points—God, man, and his brother—with two lines to make a right angle.—*Maltbie D. Babcock*.

> So many prayers, so many creeds,
> So many paths that wind and wind,
> When just the art of being kind
> Is all the sad world needs.
> —Eva Wheeler Wilcox.

I.

THE HISTORY OF THE PROPHETIC DECALOGUE.

The decalogues of Exodus 20-23 clearly represent the earliest canon of the Old Testament. These are intended to define clearly the obligations of the nation to Jehovah, and to place these obligations before the people so definitely that they would be understood and met. As the term "decalogue," that is "ten words," indicates, the Biblical decalogue originally contained ten brief sententious commands, easily memorized even by children. Each of the decalogues is divided into two groups of five laws or pentads. This division of five and ten was without reasonable doubt intended to aid the memory by associating each law with a finger or thumb of the two hands. Exodus 20-23 and its parallels in Deuteronomy contain ten decalogues, that is a decalogue of decalogues, suggesting that originally a decalogue was associated with each of the fingers and thumbs of the two hands even as were the individual words or commands. This system of mnemonics was useful in teaching a child nation. It is still useful to-day. It is important to impress upon the child in this concrete way certain of the fundamental obligations to God and man. The form of the ten commandments in part explains the commanding place which they still hold in religious education throughout Christendom.

The Biblical accounts of the two decalogues in Exodus 20 and 34 vary in details. The early Judean prophetic narrative in Exodus

34 states that these commands were inscribed by Moses himself on two stone tablets. In the later versions of the story Jehovah inscribes them with his own fingers on the two tablets which he gave to Moses. That the older decalogue was written on two tablets and set up in the temple of Solomon is exceedingly probable, for by the days of the United Kingdom the Hebrews were beginning to become acquainted with the art of writing and therefore could read the laws in written form. The recently discovered code of Hammurabi, which comes from the twentieth century B.C., was inscribed in parallel columns on a stone monument. In the epilogue to this wonderful code the king states: "By the order of Shamash, the judge supreme of heaven and earth, that judgment may shine in the land, I set up a bas-relief to preserve my likeness in the great temple that I love, to commemorate my name forever in gratitude. The oppressed who has a suit to prosecute may come before my image, that of a righteous king, and read my inscription and understand my precious words and let my stele elucidate his case. Let him see the law he seeks, and may he draw in his breath and say: 'This Hammurabi was to his people like the father that begot them!'" Thus this devout king of ancient Babylonia graphically defines the motive which, at a later period, led Israel's spiritual leaders to set before the people those principles which made for the welfare both of the nation and of the individual. Each was keenly conscious that the laws which brought social and spiritual health to mankind emanated from the divine power that was guiding the destinies of men.

Hebrew tradition has described in a great variety of narratives the way in which God made known his will to the people. The scene in each case was Mount Sinai, which the ancient Hebrews as well as the Kenites regarded as Jehovah's abode. In the early Judean version, as some writers classify the accounts, Moses alone ascends the mountain, while the people are forbidden to approach. In the Northern Israelite version, the people approach, but being terrified by the thunder and lightnings they request Moses to receive for them the divine message. This later version implies that a raging thunder storm shrouded the sacred mountain, while the early Judean and late priestly narratives apparently suggest an active volcano.

The element common to all these accounts is that under the direction of their prophetic leader, Moses, a solemn covenant was established between the nation and Jehovah, and that the obligations of the people were defined in the decalogue with its ten short commands. The problem is, however, complicated by the presence of two decalogues, one now preserved in Exodus 34 and the other, the familiar ten commandments of Exodus 20. Both agree in emphasizing as primary the nation's obligation to be loyal to Jehovah. The decalogue in Exodus 34, however, goes on to describe in succeeding laws the ways in which the nation may show its loyalty. This was through the observation of certain ceremonial customs and especially the great annual feasts. Did most ancient peoples show their loyalty to the gods by their lives and deeds or by the ceremonies of the ritual and the offerings which they brought to the altars? The first great prophet Amos declared that Jehovah hated and despised feasts and ceremonies unless accompanied by deeds of justice and mercy.

The decalogue in Exodus 34 may well represent the original commands which Moses laid upon the nation, but the higher moral sense of later editors has truly recognized the superiority of the ethical commands of the familiar decalogue in Exodus 20 and given it the commanding place which it richly deserves. (For a probable literary history of this decalogue see *Hist. Bible* I, 194-5.) The two decalogues of Exodus 20 and 34 are not duplicates the one of the other, but rather supplement each other. The one defines the obligation of the nation, the other of the individual. The Hebrews long continued to retain in their homes the family images inherited from their Semitic ancestors. Not until the days of Amos and Isaiah did the prophets begin to protest against the calves or bulls and the cherubim in the sanctuaries of Northern Israel, and even in the temple at Jerusalem. Hence the second command, "Thou shalt not make for thyself any graven image," some believe comes from a period centuries later than Moses. Possibly, as in Exodus 34:17, it originally read "molten image" and referred to foreign idols. If so, it may come in this older form from Moses. The tenth command which places the emphasis on the motive rather than the act also suggests a maturer age; but with these possible exceptions there is good reason for believing that the spirit and teaching of Moses are embodied in this noble decalogue.

In what respects does the version in Deuteronomy 5 differ from that in Exodus 20? *(Hist. Bible* I, 195.) Which is probably the older version? What later explanations and exhortations have been added to the original ten words in Exodus 20? In Deuteronomy 5? What was the object of these additions? Are they of real value? Is it profitable to teach them to children to-day?

II.

OBLIGATIONS OF THE INDIVIDUAL TO GOD.

Into what two groups do the ten words in Exodus 20 fall? And what is the theme of each? Is there a real difference between the command of Exodus 34, "Thou shalt worship no other gods" and that of Exodus 20, "Thou shall have no other gods before me"? Did the Hebrews as a matter of fact tolerate the worship of other gods in their midst centuries after the days of Moses? May the Hebrews have originally interpreted the command of Exodus 20 as a demand that Jehovah be given the first place in the worship and faith of Israel? How did later prophets like Elijah and Isaiah interpret it? (See I Kings 18:21 and Is. 6:1-8; 8:13.) The older command in Exodus 34, "Thou shall make thee no molten gods," was probably intended to guard the Israelites from imitating the religious customs of their heathen neighbors, such as the Egyptians and the Moabites. The command to make no graven image was, it seems, directed not against the public idols but against the private images. These were usually made of wood and were cherished in many a Hebrew family, as for example, that of Jacob (cf. the story of his flight from Laban, Gen. 31) or of David (I Sam. 19). The spirit of the law is truly interpreted by the later priestly commentator who places completely under the ban all attempts visibly to represent the Deity. Is the spirit of this command disregarded by the modern Greek church? In certain parts of the Roman Catholic world? In any phases of Protestant worship?

How is the third command interpreted to-day? The exact meaning of the original Hebrew is not entirely clear. It may be interpreted literally: "Thou shall not invoke the name of Jehovah, thy God, in vain." The interpretation turns on the meaning of the phrase, in vain. This admits of four different translations: (1) Purposelessly, and therefore needlessly or irreverently; (2) for destruction, as when a man calls down a curse upon another; (3)

for nothing, that is in swearing to what is not true; and (4) in the practice of sorcery or witchcraft, for this word was frequently used by the Hebrews as a scornful designation of heathen abominations. Is it possible that the original command was intended to guard against each of these evils? If so, it broadens and deepens its modern application. Its fundamental idea is evidently reverence and sincerity.

Why did the Hebrew law-givers place these three laws, which emphasize absolute loyalty to Jehovah, at the beginning of the decalogue? What do we mean to-day by loyalty to God? Loyalty to Jehovah was not only the corner stone of Israel's religion but also of the Hebrew state. During the wilderness period and far down into later periods it was the chief and at times practically the only bond that bound together the individual members of the tribe and nation. Disloyalty to Jehovah was treason, and even the mild code found in the book of Deuteronomy directs that apostasy be punished by public stoning. Loyalty to God or at least to the individual sense of right to-day as in the past is the first essential of effective citizenship. Which is the more essential for the welfare of the state, the manual, the mental or the religious training of its citizens? Where is the chief emphasis placed to-day? Is this right?

III.

THE SOCIAL AND ETHICAL BASIS OF THE SABBATH LAW.

The institution of the Sabbath in different countries apparently has a long and complex history. Many explanations have been given of its origin, aside from the direct divine command. The simplest and most satisfactory is probably that it was originally connected with the worship of the moon. There are many indications in Hebrew history that the early ancestors of the Israelites were moon worshippers. To-day as in the distant past the inhabitants of the deserts from whence came the forefathers of the Hebrews make their journeys under the clear, cool light of the moon, avoiding the hot, piercing rays of the mid-day sun. The moon with its marvelous transformations is unquestionably the most striking and awe-inspiring object in the heavens. It is not strange, therefore, that many primitive peoples and especially the nomadic desert dwellers worshipped it as the supreme embodiment of beauty and power.

In China feast days once a month were doubtless connected with the phases of the moon. Among the American Indians time was reckoned by numbers of moons. The custom of observing as sacred the four days, which marked the transition from one quarter of the moon to another, was also widespread. In the Hebrew religion the feast of the New Moon was closely identified with that of the Sabbath. The Hebrew month was also the lunar month of approximately twenty-eight days. The new moon, therefore, marked the beginning of the month and each succeeding Sabbath a new phase of the moon. The fourth commandment seems, therefore, like the others to have a basis in nature, and also, as we shall note, a social reason. Would a commandment be truly divine if it did not have a natural and reasonable basis? By the ancients rest from labor was regarded as one of the essential elements in the sacred day. The prophet Amos denounced the merchants of Northern Israel because they were constantly saying,

> When shall the new moon pass that we may sell grain,
> And the Sabbath that we may open the corn?

In its earlier ceremonial interpretation, to abstain from all labor on the Sabbath was clearly regarded as a primary obligation. Like fasting, it is probably regarded as an offering due to Jehovah. The word "holy" in the Hebrew means set apart, distinct. The Sabbath, therefore, was to differ from the other days of the week. The great ethical prophets of the Assyrian period were the first completely to divest this ancient institution of its heathen significance and give it a deeper religious, and therefore social and humanitarian interpretation. They gave it its true and eternal content, declaring that God decreed that all who labor should have their needed rest. The prophet who added the noble interpretation in Deuteronomy 5:14, 15, declares that it was not only that old and young, master and slave, might rest, but also that even the toiling ox and ass and the resident alien might have the relaxation which their tired bodies required. Thus these inspired prophets traced the ultimate basis of the institution of the Sabbath to God's providence for the innate needs of man. They recognized that it was essential for the physical, mental and spiritual well-being of the individual and, therefore, for the welfare of the State. That the Hebrews might not forget this obligation, the prophets appealed to the memory of the days when the Israelites themselves were slaves in the land of Egypt and the thought of how Jehovah delivered them from their slavery.

Tuan Fang, the great Manchu viceroy who only recently met martyrdom at the hands of his warring countrymen, said when visiting America a few years ago, "I think that when I return to China I will introduce Sunday in my province." When asked whether he would make it the seventh day, he replied, "Yes, for I think that the seventh day is far better than the tenth. Furthermore, for the convenience and economy of all, I will make it correspond to the Christian Sunday. From my study of the conditions in America and of the needs in China I am convinced that the Sabbath is a most valuable and essential institution."

Later Judaism revived the earlier heathen content of the Sabbath, and lost sight of its deeper political, social and humanitarian significance. Unfortunately the Christian church and above all our Puritan fathers followed the guidance of the later priests rather than of the early prophets. Jesus with his clear insight into human hearts and needs, and with his glowing love for men, repudiated the harsh, mechanical interpretation of the Sabbath current in his day and reasserted the teachings of the great prophets that preceded him; "The Sabbath was made for man, not man for the Sabbath."

Does the social and humanitarian interpretation of the Sabbath obscure or deepen its religious significance? Does the great body of the Christian church to-day accept the interpretation of the prophets and of Jesus, or that of early heathenism and later Judaism? Does the interpretation of the prophets and of Jesus furnish a basis on which all classes in the state can unite in appreciating and in jealously guarding the Sabbath? Does the acceptance of one or the other of these interpretations fundamentally affect our actual observance of the Sabbath? Our motives and our spirit? Our attitude toward our fellow men?

IV.

IMPORTANCE OF CHILDREN'S LOYALTY TO PARENTS

It is generally recognized by scientists that the place of animals in the scale of being is dependent upon the length of their period of infancy. The lower forms of animal life are mature almost as soon as they are born. Minnows never come under the care of their genitors, but are independent as soon as they are hatched. The young of the less developed quadrupeds are soon weaned and forgotten by their parents. The longer the young remain in the care of their parents the higher the form of the animal. The great difference between men and most of the higher animals is thought by many to be dependent upon the length of childhood, and the consequent care and attention given by the parents. Even among human beings it is scarcely too much to say that the longer the time of education and training under proper supervision lasts, the more successful finally at the end of life the man will be. When one considers that Aristotle, who is perhaps generally accepted as the world's greatest thinker, associated with his great teacher, Plato, twenty years, until he was thirty-eight years of age and produced nearly all his important works only after that time, we may see one example of the profound importance of training. The care of parents for their children throughout all of their early years would naturally imply loyalty of children to the parents as a mark of gratitude for the time and affection expended upon them.

In one of his characteristic poems, filled with wise suggestion, Lowell speaks of obedience as that "great tap root" of the state and civilization. The habit of obedience is one of the finest characteristics in family life, and obedience to parents normally becomes obedience to law in the citizen, one of the surest bonds of society and one of the most necessary conditions of social progress.

This fact was so fully recognized in the patriarchal stage of society that the head of the family within the tribe had the power even of life and death over the members of his household. In practically all early societies we find this authority of the parent and the obedience of the child insisted upon as fundamental. In the

Orient, even to the present day, this respect of children for their parents is closely bound up with their religion and their civilization. The first wish of every man is that be may have a son to sacrifice to his memory after he has gone. And not only in China, but in many other states we find ancestral worship springing from this relation of father and son.

The primitive Hebrew laws (Ex. 21:15, 17) made death the penalty for a child who struck or cursed his parents. In many countries parricide is considered the worse type of murder. The very old Sumerian law of ancient Babylon punished with slavery the son who repudiated his father. In the fifth commandment no penalty is named for disrespect toward one's parents. The religious sanction only is implied, though the penalty of death was inflicted by the law of the tribe.

In society to-day our aim in education is to develop individuality and for a country with a democratic form of government this type of education should be encouraged. Disobedience or disrespect ho parents has no longer a legal penalty, although the children may be compelled by law to support their parents. But gratitude toward parents and a normal affectionate family life are practically essential to social welfare. Aside from its civic aspect, there is nothing in society more beautiful than the right relationship between parents and children. Jesus, who represented the kingdom of God as a household, found that the best analogy for the relationship of men to God and the best descriptions of the divine nature are based upon this relationship.

V.

PRIMARY OBLIGATIONS OF MAN TO MAN.

The second five commandments of the decalogue deal with the obligations of man to man. These commands still find a central place in modern society as the best guarantees of social stability, security and peace. All of the crimes with which they deal, except that of covetousness, were punished, in Hebrew custom and law, by definite penalties. In many instances these penalties were still more severe among other early peoples.

As soon as society emerges from the savage state, the crime of adultery is always forbidden. Nothing else stirs the worst of human passions as does sexual jealousy. Even to-day probably no other cause is more productive of murder and suicide. In early societies, like that of the Israelites, to this normal human feeling of personal wrong was added that of the loss of property, for wives or concubines were considered as property. Hence the penalty for adultery among the Hebrews, as with many ancient and many modern peoples, was death.

As soon as society develops from the savage into the pastoral stage, private property is recognized in the flocks and herds. In the development of society additional types of property rights appear under various forms of ownership, until it is not too much to say that modern society is based largely upon property rights. The evils associated with property are many, but as yet, at any rate, the rights of property are a benefit to the state, provided those rights are exercised under proper legal supervision. It should be recognized, however, that the command, "Thou shall not steal," may well have various meanings, dependent upon the laws of property. Our law restricts the right of legacy, the sale or even the possession of poisons and often of dangerous weapons. Similarly the degree of ownership of other goods is often limited.

The ninth command, not to bear false witness against one's neighbor, is often interpreted as simply a violation of one's oath in court, or when appended to formal legal papers. But in most modern countries the command is also interpreted so as to include lying. If this crime is defined in its broadest sense, as lack of truth and trustworthiness, it is in many ways the greatest sin man can commit against society. Practically all modern economic and social relations are based upon the security of contracts and upon the readiness of business men and citizens to keep their word. It may be well questioned whether the crime of murder is as dangerous to society as the habit of deception, for the temptation of murder is rare as compared with that of deception; while the evil is often less far-reaching in its consequence and less despicable.

In the last command, that directed against covetousness, the law-giver goes beyond the external act to the motive and spirit in the mind of the individual. If this command is kept in spirit, the others are practically unnecessary. This command is like in kind to that of Jesus in the New Testament, where all the commandments are summed up into one: "Love one another."

VI.

THE PRESENT-DAY AUTHORITY OF THE TEN COMMANDMENTS.

The various books that make up our Bible were each written to meet the needs of the people of its day; but inasmuch as the prophets and law-givers from the days of Moses to those of Jesus touched upon the most vital questions of human life and society, these principles are most of them universal and applicable to all tribes and nations and races and peoples.

Necessarily there are many variations in the specific methods by which these commands are to be carried out. The honor and reverence due everywhere to mother and father may well have different applications, depending upon the type of civilization, the customs of living and the type of home life that exist in the different countries. The injunction to keep the Sabbath may well be carried out with the same spirit in various ways. What constitutes theft depends upon the law of the separate state and upon the rights of property granted by that law, but everywhere the primary obligations of the individual to God, to society and to his fellow men remain substantially the same. As he develops a more tender conscience, a more just and kindly attitude toward his fellows, a greater reverence toward his Creator, the spirit with which be keeps these commandments is becoming continually more urgent, whatever may be the specific way in which they may be carried out for the benefit of his fellow men and of society.

Questions for Further Consideration.

Does idol worship exist in any part of the civilized world today? If so, where and in what forms?

Are those addicted to profanity necessarily and intentionally irreverent? What is the origin of this habit? How may it be eradicated? What are some of the best methods by which children may be guarded against it?

Do you think it is right for the state to become responsible for the religious education of its citizens?

What is the fundamental difference between the so-called "Continental Sabbath" and that observed by Jesus?

In what way may Sunday be made a day of greater profit and significance to the working man?

What attitude should one take regarding so-called "white" or "society lies"? Under what circumstances, if any, is it right to lie?

Subjects for Further Study.

(1) The Decalogues in Exodus 20-23. *Hist. Bible* II, 209-24.
(2) Jesus' Version of the Ancient Prophetic Decalogue. See Matt. 5:17, 18; 6:19-21; 12:1-12, 31, 32; 15:3-5; 22: 36-39.
(3) Compare the Moral Ideals of the Decalogue with those of the Present-Day Socialists. Cross, *The Essentials of Socialism*; Walling, *Socialism as It Is*; Spargo, *Elements of Socialism*.

STUDY XI

THE EARLY TRAINING OF A RACE.

ISRAEL'S EXPERIENCE IN THE WILDERNESS AND EAST OF THE JORDAN—Num. 11-14; 21:21-31; 32:39-42.

Parallel Readings.

Hist. Bible I, 204-29.
Edward Jenks, Hist. of Politics, Chap, III.

Then as they journeyed from the mountain of Jehovah the ark of Jehovah went before them, to seek out a halting place for them. And whenever the ark started, Moses would say,

> Arise, O Jehovah,
> And let thine enemies be scattered,
> And let those who hate thee flee before thee.

And when it rested, he would say,
Return, O Jehovah, to the ten thousand of thousands of Israel.—*Num. 10:33, 35, 36.*

As an eagle stirreth up her nest, hovereth over her young, taketh them, beareth them upon her wings, so the Lord his God did lead him and there was no strange God with him.—*Deut. 32: 11.*

Before man made us citizens, great Nature made us men—
Lowell.

> Oh, East is East, and West is West, and never the twain
>   shall meet
> Till earth and sky stand presently at God's great judgment
>   seat;
> But there is neither East, nor West, border nor breed nor
>   birth
> When two strong men stand face to face, tho' they come
>   from the ends of the earth.
>   —Rudyard Kipling.

The measure of the success of our lives can only lie in the stature of our manhood, in the growth in unworldliness and in the moral elevation of our inner self.—*Henry Drummond.*

I.

THE WILDERNESS ENVIRONMENT.

The accounts regarding the experiences of the Israelites in the wilderness lack the unity which characterizes the records of the earlier and later periods. They simply give occasional pictures of the life of the Hebrew fugitives. They must be interpreted in the light of the peculiar background of the wilderness and of the nomadic life which flourishes there to-day as it did in the past. The Hebrews on escaping from Egypt entered the South Country, which extends seventy miles from the rocky hills of Judah southward until it merges into the barren desert. During the later Roman period the northern and northwestern portions of this territory were partially reclaimed by agriculturalists; but in early periods, as to-day, it was pre-eminently the home of wandering, nomadic tribes. This wild, treeless region is divided by rocky ranges running from east to west. Parallel to these are deep, hot and for the most part waterless valleys. In the springtime these valleys are covered by a sparse vegetation; from a few perennial springs flow waters that irrigate the immediately surrounding land; but they soon lose themselves in the thirsty desert. During the summer the vegetation disappears almost entirely, and the struggle for subsistence becomes intense. The nature of the country makes it necessary for its inhabitants constantly to journey from one pasture land and spring to another.

The home of the Hebrews at this time, like that of the modern Arabs, was the tent. The stories that have come down from this period suggest the experiences through which they passed. The constant insistent problem in this region was and is how to secure adequate supplies of food and water. During the greater part of the year the chief food of the people is the milk and curds supplied by their herds. At times, however, these fail to meet the needs even of the modern Bedouin inhabitants of this South Country. They then gather the gum that exudes from the tamarisk tree or the lichens from the rocks. From these they make a coarse flour and bread which keeps them alive until the winter rains again bring their supply of water and pasturage. Some scholars hold that this coarse food was the manna of the Biblical accounts. They argue that later generations, familiar with the barrenness of the wilderness and believing that the Hebrews at this time numbered many thousands, naturally concluded and reported that their ancestors were miraculously fed. At certain periods, also, the meagre fare of the desert dweller is supplemented by the quails which he is able to capture and these are a welcome relief to his monotonous diet. About the perennial springs, which gush forth from the barren rock, there also grew up stories of a miraculous provision for the needs of Jehovah's people; for all springs and especially those in the desert were regarded by the ancients as miracles. Even in more fertile lands the Greeks reared beside such springs temples to the god, whom they thought of as thus signally revealing himself. In the deeper sense each of these early Hebrew stories is historical, for they all record the fundamental thought and belief that through this strenuous, painful period, even as in later crises in their history, Jehovah was guiding his people and giving them not only food and water, but also that training in the school of danger and privation which was essential for their highest development.

Even more insistent than the constant struggle for food and water were the dangers that came from the hostile tribes which already occupied this much-contested territory. For the possession of the springs and pasture lands they fought with the energy and craft that characterize the Bedouin tribes to-day. Hence, to the Hebrews, fresh from the fertile fields of Egypt, their life in the wilderness represented constant hardship, privation, suffering and danger.

II.

INFLUENCE OV THE NOMADIC LIFE UPON ISRAEL'S CHARACTER AND IDEALS.

The wilderness left a stamp upon Hebrew character and life that may be traced even to-day in the later descendants of that race. It tightened their muscles and gave them that physical virility which has enabled them to survive even amidst the most unfavorable conditions. It taught them how to subsist on the most meagre food supply and to thrive where the citizen of a more prosperous land would inevitably starve.

It is probable that in their early nomadic experiences the Hebrews acquired those migratory habits which, intensified by unwonted vicissitudes, have carried them to almost every civilized land. In the wilderness they also learned the art of nomadic warfare which, to win victories, depended not so much upon open attack as upon strategy. The common dangers of the wilderness life tightened the racial and religious bonds that held them together. Only by the closest union could they resist the perils that beset them. Upon the complete devotion of each man to the interest of the tribe hung his fate, as well as that of the community as a whole. Hence arose that devotion to race, that readiness to avenge every wrong and to protect each individual, even if it cost the life-blood of the tribe, which is illustrated in many of the stories that come from this early period. How far has this racial characteristic survived?

In a community thus closely bound together the morality of each individual was guarded with a jealousy unknown in more settled prosperous communities. Thus, for example, adultery from the first appears to have been punished by public stoning. How far has this characteristic survived to the glory of the Jewish race?

The tribal organization also cherished the freedom of each individual. His voice was heard in its council and his rights were carefully protected. The free atmosphere of the desert tolerated no despotism, and the sheik was the servant of all. These fundamental conceptions of government persisted even when, under the influence of a new agricultural environment, the Hebrews established the kingship and monarchy. It was the struggle between these inherited democratic ideals and those of the neighbors who were ruled by despots, that ultimately disrupted the Hebrew kingdom and called forth those great champions of liberty and social justice, the prophets of the Assyrian period. It was this same democratic atmosphere that made possible the work of those prophets, who openly denounced the crimes of king and people. How far have the Jews throughout all their history allied themselves with democratic movements?

III.

THE INFLUENCE OF THE WILDERNESS LIFE UPON ISRAEL'S FAITH.

The pressure of constant danger intensified the sense of dependence upon a power outside and above themselves. It led them to look constantly to Jehovah as their sole guide and deliverer. A continued attitude crystallized into a habit. Hence, throughout their troubled career the Hebrews have been conscious of the presence of God and have found in him their defender and personal friend as has no other people in human history.

As later generations meditated on the perils of the wilderness through which their ancestors passed, they naturally felt that only under the immediate guidance of a divine power could they have escaped. They were familiar with the way in which the caravans travel through the desert: in front of the leader is borne aloft a brazier filled with coals. From this smouldering fire there arises by day a column of smoke that, in the clear air of the desert, can be easily seen afar by any who may straggle behind. At night these glowing coals seem like a pillar of fire, telling of the presence of their leader and protector. With the same vivid imagery, according to some interpreters, the later Hebrews pictured the march of their ancestors through the wilderness, and thereby symbolized the belief that Jehovah was then present and that through his prophet Moses he was personally guiding his people. How far have these Old Testament narratives been thus interpreted by modern western readers? Does it change their spiritual significance to seek to learn their origin and real literary character? Are there still to be found, often in humble walks of life, earnest Christians who have similar deep spiritual experiences and describe them with the same vivid imagery and concreteness? Is the value of our conception of God's presence and activity in human history deepened and strengthened or lessened by the thought that in the past, even as today, he accomplished his ends by natural rather than contra-natural methods? Are the faith and institutions of nations and individuals developed most through special revelations or through ordinary, constant, daily training and experience? Is it not true that to us all there come at times experiences akin to those that underlie these wonderful narratives?

IV.

THE SIGNIFICANCE OF THE EAST-JORDAN CONQUESTS.

Desert dwellers take little account of the lapse of time. It is not strange that the data regarding the duration of the sojourn in the wilderness are late and exceedingly vague. The number forty in the Bible is the concrete Hebrew equivalent of many. Ordinarily the forty years represent a generation. A period of about forty years accords well with the facts of contemporary Egyptian chronology. If the Hebrews fled from Egypt about 1200, during the period of anarchy following the breakdown of the nineteenth Egyptian dynasty, they could not have entered Palestine much before the middle of the twelfth century, for Ramses III of the Twentieth Dynasty succeeded in re-establishing and maintaining his authority in Southern Palestine until his death about 1167 B.C.

The account of the spies, preserved according to some writers in variant versions by each of the great groups of Hebrew narratives, indicates that the Hebrews attempted but failed to enter Canaan from the south. For tribesmen like the Israelites, chafing under their harsh environment and recalling the prosperity of the land of Egypt, Palestine with its green hills and fertile fields was an irresistible lodestone luring them on to the conquest.

The reasons why they failed to enter Canaan from the south are suggested in the narrative of the spies and confirmed by a study of the historical geographical situation. The Canaanite cities of Southern Palestine were built largely with the view to protecting their inhabitants from the ever-lurking nomad invaders. On the other hand the Hebrews had none of the equipment needed to conquer walled cities. More than that the barren hills of the South Country did not furnish the base of supplies necessary to maintain a protracted siege. The early Hebrew narratives imply that certain nomadic tribes, as, for example, the Calebites, the Kenizzites and the Jerahmeelites, independently gained a foothold on the southern borders of Canaan and ultimately assimilated with the Hebrew tribe of Judah when the latter entered Palestine. The earliest Hebrew accounts, however, as well as the logic of the situation indicate that the great body of the Israelites, whose ancestors had been in the land of Egypt, entered Palestine from the east. Throughout all its history the east-Jordan land has witnessed the constant transition of Arab tribes from the nomadic life of the desert to the more settled civilization, of agricultural Palestine. Here on the eastern heights that overlook the Jordan valley and the land of Canaan the traveller still finds the Arab tents and flocks of the nomads beside the plowed fields of the village-dwellers. On the rolling plains of northern Moab and southern Gilead there are few commanding heights or natural fortresses. The important towns, like Dibon and Heshbon, lay on slightly rising hills. The character of the ruins today does not indicate that they were ever surrounded by formidable walls. Whether the Hebrews conquered them by open attack or by strategy, as in the case of the town of Ai, is not stated. It is certain, however, that here they first gained a permanent foothold in agricultural Palestine. From the conquered they here learned their initial lessons in the arts of agriculture and became acquainted with that more advanced Canaanite civilization which they later absorbed. Coming fresh from the desert, where only the fittest survived, their numbers rapidly increased in this quieter and more favorable environment. Soon to the constant pressure of the desert population on the east was added that of over-population, so that necessity, as well as ambition, impelled them to cross the Jordan to seek homes among the hills to the west.

V.

THE SIGNIFICANCE OF MOSES' WORK.

The study of the beginnings of Israel's history in the light of its physical, social and economic environment reveals clearly the many powerful forces then at work. At the same time these do not alone explain Israel's later history and the uniqueness of its character and faith. These later facts plainly point back to a strong, commanding personality, who shaped the ideals and institutions of this early people and left upon them the imperishable imprint of his own unique individuality. Although the traditions regarding him have been transmitted for centuries from mouth to mouth, they portray the character and work of Moses with remarkable clarity and impressiveness. Moses was primarily a patriot. He was also a prophet-statesman, able to grasp and interpret the significance of the great crises in the life of his people and to suggest practical solutions. Moreover, he was able to inspire confidence, and to lead as well as direct. In the harsh environment of the wilderness he was able to adjust himself to most difficult conditions. In leading the Hebrew serfs from the land of Egypt, he became indeed the creator of the future Hebrew nation. In the wilderness be trained that child nation. As judge and counsellor, he taught concretely the broad principles which became the foundation of later Hebrew law.

As guardian of the oracle and priest of the desert sanctuary, Moses, like the later prophet of Islam, but with far greater spiritual power and deeper insight, taught his people not only the art of worship, but certain of the great essentials of religion. He it was who formulated in a positive faith the wholesome reaction, which he and his kinsmen felt against the gross polytheism of Egypt. The inspiration of all of Moses' work was his own personal faith. The first great vision of Jehovah's character and purpose that he had received in the land of Midian was doubtless often renewed amidst the same wild, impressive scenes. The exact nature of the deeper, more personal side of his character and faith must be inferred from the close analogies that may be drawn from the memoirs of Isaiah or Jeremiah. At the same time it is a mistake to infer that Moses' beliefs were as lofty as those of the later prophets who stood in the light of a larger experience. On the other hand, it is not just to disregard the fact that Moses, being a prophet, was far in advance of the primitive age in which he lived. Not only did Moses create the Hebrew nation and teach it its first lessons in practical politics and religion, but he it was who first instilled into his race commanding loyalty to the one God, Jehovah, and taught that religion was more than form: that it meant right thinking and doing. Thus Moses was the forerunner of Israel's later prophets, who broke away from the narrow heathen interpretation of religion and defined it in terms of life and service.

VI.

THE EARLY STAGES IN THE TRAINING OF THE HUMAN RACE.

It is interesting and important to note that Israel's history was in most respects like that of other growing nations. In the beginning pastoral society and tribal government develop among savages primarily through the domestication of animals. The young of the animals slain in the hunt are kept first as pets: then, when as a result of the thriftless nature of the savages supplies at times become scarce, the pets are slain for food. As pets become more common and population increases, the advantage of breeding for use is apparent, and private property, in distinction from community possessions, appears. The growing herds naturally develop the need of regular service. To meet this need the institutions of permanent marriage and bondage arise and the wife or wives and the slaves perform the added work. With the custom of fixed marriage and the possibility of tracing ancestry through the father, comes in time ancestral government. The Hebrews seem to have had this type of government, even in the days of Abraham; and it lasted until the tribes broke up into clans and families, when they acquired permanent homes and became agriculturists in the land of Canaan.

Many of the characteristics of the tribe disappear almost entirely, as wandering nomads settle in a fixed abode, and the patriarchal rule changes to that of a royal or democratic government. Customs become fixed in formal statutes. Property in land becomes more important than that in herds. War becomes the business of a special army, instead of the frequent duty of all.

But in the tribe there is little competition. All work for the community, or for the family, rather than for individual interests. Each man is primarily responsible, not to the state, but to the head of his family or clan, who in turn answers for his family to the tribal chief.

Certain of these tribal institutions and ideals have left their indelible impress on modern society. The tribe was exclusive. All those not born into the tribe had no right, no welcome there, for their coming would tend to restrict the common pasturage. They would be a burden. Though the tent-dweller might be hospitable to a guest, an alien had no rights except on sufferance. If he were needy and were received, he usually became a serf or slave. And yet this exclusiveness is the germ of our patriotism, a noble trait that may ultimately, but not soon, be replaced by a cosmopolitan love for humanity.

Allied to this is the personal bond, that obtains in the tribe, instead of the territorial unity of the modern state. A Frenchman is such because he is born in France; an Israelite is such because he is the son of Abraham and knows his people as his blood kinsmen.

This personal tie makes for peace and democracy. Building on this Jewish tribal trait, Jesus calls all men brethren because sons of a common Father. His Kingdom of God, likewise, is not territorial. Its citizens are bound together by the tribal bond of a common brotherhood and fatherhood. Thus the lessons, so deeply impressed in the childhood of the race, have a large and growing significance for the present and future.

Questions for Further Consideration.

What reasons may be given to prove that love for humanity is a virtue more useful to modern civilization than patriotism?

Does the movement for universal peace find any encouragement in the teachings ascribed to Moses?

On what grounds can the conquest of Canaan by the Israelites be defended? How did it differ from the taking of Tripoli by Italy? Or of Porto Rico by the United States?

In the light of the oldest records, was Moses' work in your judgment accomplished by natural or supernatural methods?

What were the chief characteristics of Moses? What place does he hold in history?

Is modern socialism in any way a revival of the principles underlying the old tribal organization? How far did Jesus in his idea of the Kingdom of God build on the old tribal idea?

Subjects/ or Further Study.

(1) Characteristics of the Wilderness South of Palestine. Hastings, *Dict. Bib.* III, 505-6. Kent, *Bib. Geog. and Hist.*, 42, 43.
(2) The Religion of Moses. Hastings, *Dict. Bib.*, Extra Vol. 631-634; Marti, *Old Testament Religion*, 36-71.
(3) Compare the tribal organization and customs of the Israelites with those of the American Indian tribes of to-day. Publications of the *Indian Association*; publications of the *Mohonk Conferences.*

STUDY XII

A NATION'S STRUGGLE FOR A HOME AND FREEDOM.

ISRAEL'S VICTORIES OVER THE CANAANITES.—Josh. 2-9; Judg. 1, 4, 5.

Parallel Readings.

Hist. Bible II,1-4.1.
Prin. of Politics X.

That the leaders took the lead in Israel,
That the people volunteered readily,
Bless Jehovah!

Zebulun was a people who exposed themselves to deadly peril,
And Naphtali on the heights of the open field.
Kings came, they fought;
They fought, the kings of Canaan,
At Taanach by the Waters of Megiddo,
They took no booty of silver.
Prom heaven fought the stars,
From their courses fought against Sisera,
The river Kishon swept them away,
That ancient river, the river Kishon.
O my soul, march on with strength!

> When did the horse-hoofs resound
> With the galloping, galloping of their steeds?
> —Judg. 5, 9, 18-22 (Hist. Bible).

This was King Arthur's dreame. Him thought that there was comen into his lande many gryffons and serpents, and him thought that they brent and slew all the people in the land. And then him thought that he fought with them, and they did him passing great damage and wounded him full sore, but at the last he slewe them all.—Malory, *Hist. of King Arthur, Mort d' Arthur.*

Young gentlemen, have a resolute life purpose. Don't get mad and don't get scared.—*Burleson.*

I.

THE CROSSING OF THE JORDAN.

In the light of the preceding studies, the motives that led the Hebrews to cross the Jordan become evident. As the Pilgrim Fathers, to secure a home where they might enjoy and develop their own type of belief and methods of civilization, braved the dimly known dangers of the sea and the wilderness, the Hebrews braved the contests that unquestionably lay before them. Between the Sea of Galilee and the Dead Sea the Jordan is fordable at thirty points during certain parts of the year. The first of the two main fords in the lower Jordan is just below the point where the Wady Kelt enters the Jordan from the west and deposits its mass of mud and silt. The other ford is six miles further north below the point where the Wady Nimrin comes down from the highlands of Gilead. Here to-day the main highway connecting the east and the west-Jordan country crosses the river. This spot was probably the scene of the historic crossing at the beginning of Hebrew history.

Certain writers hold that variant accounts of the most important facts in early Hebrew history have here been preserved. Traces of three different versions of the crossing of the Jordan may still, in their judgment, be found in the third and fourth chapters of the book of Joshua. The latest and most familiar narrative represents the crossing as a superlative miracle and the waters of the rushing river as piled up like a wall on either side. The

Northern Israelite version appears to have stated that the waters of the Jordan were dried up, implying that the Hebrews crossed during the late summer when the river was easily fordable. The earliest narrative, the Judean prophetic, states that "the waters rose up in a heap, a great way off at Adam, the city that is beside Zarathan, and those that went down toward the Sea of the Arabah, the Salt Sea, were wholly cut off" (Josh. 3:16b). From other references in the Old Testament it would appear that the city of Adam, which means red earth, is to-day represented by the ruins of Ed-Damieh, which stands near the famous Damieh ford at the point where the river Jabbok enters the Jordan.

It is interesting to note in this connection that a reliable Moslem historian states that in the year 1257 A.D. the retreating Moslems found it neccessary to repair the foundations of an important bridge which stood at this point. When the workmen arrived on the scene they were amazed to find the riverbed empty and were able by working rapidly to complete the repairs before the waters came rushing down. This remarkable phenomenon seemed to them to be due to the direct intervention of Allah; but the historian fortunately records the cause: it was a huge landslide a little further up the river which temporarily dammed its waters. The oldest Biblical account of the crossing of the Jordan may point to a like natural cause. If this be true, does it imply that Jehovah had no part in preparing the way for the future conquests of his people? Would a miracle, such as that recorded in the late-priestly tradition, be any stronger proof of God's presence and activity in human history than are the provisions which we to-day call natural?

II.

THE CANAANITE CIVILIZATION.

Contemporary inscriptions and recent excavations make it possible to form a very definite conception of conditions in Canaan when the Hebrews crossed the Jordan. The dominant civilization was that of the Canaanites, the descendants of the Semitic invaders from the desert who entered Palestine centuries before the ancestors of the Hebrews. Naturally they settled first along the fertile coast plains that skirt the western Mediterranean.

In later times these were known as the Phoenicians. As the population increased, the Canaanites pushed their outposts along the broad valleys that penetrated the uplands of Palestine. These valleys were especially fertile and attractive in the territory later known as Galilee and Samaria. The wide Plain of Esdraelon and its eastward extension, the Valley of Jezreel, cut straight across the central plateau of Palestine. The Plain of Esdraelon was the strongest centre of the Canaanite civilization. A few outposts were established in the Jordan valley, as for example, Laish, later known as Dan, at the foot of Mount Hermon, and Jericho, at the southern end of the Jordan valley. Only a few Canaanite villages were found along the more barren hills of Southern Canaan. There the peoples and civilization still retained the imprint of their desert origin.

Along the coast plains and across the great Plain of Esdraelon ran the main highways that connected the three earliest and most nourishing centres of the world's civilization: the Egyptian on the southwest, the Amorite on the north, probably between the southern Lebanons, and the Babylonian to the east and northeast. For centuries the Canaanites had absorbed the ideas, institutions, and culture of these stronger peoples. So fundamentally had the Babylonians impressed the Canaanites that practically all of the inscriptions coming from this early period are written in the Babylonian script. Even in writing to their Egyptian conqueror during the fourteenth century, the Canaanite kings of Palestine used this same Babylonian system of writing. The Amorite civilization had so strongly influenced the Canaanites that to-day it is difficult for the archaeologist to distinguish between the two. By certain of the Biblical writers the terms Canaanite and Amorite are used interchangeably. As early as 1600 B.C. Egypt, under the ambitious conquering kings of the Eighteenth Dynasty, had overrun Palestine and for the next three or four centuries ruled it as a tributary province. The nearness of Egypt made its influence still more powerful, so that in nearly every mound and Canaanite ruin the excavator finds hundreds of reminders of the presence of the Egyptian civilization.

The Canaanites had long since left behind them the nomadic state and had developed a strong agricultural and commercial civilization. Their life centered about certain important cities like Megiddo on the southwestern side and Bethshean on the eastern side of the Plain of Esdraelon. Their cities were usually built on a low-lying hill in the midst of rich encircling plains. They were provided with thick mud walls, behind which the inhabitants felt secure from attack. Over each city ruled a petty king, whose authority, however, did not extend far beyond the surrounding fields that belonged to the inhabitants of the town. Generally these city states were independent. In many cases they were hostile to each other; and the long rule of Egypt had tended to intensify this hostility, for Egypt had depended upon this local jealousy to maintain its control. The diversified physical contour of Palestine likewise strengthened this tendency toward separation rather than unity.

This type of political organization favored the growth of polytheism rather than the worship of one god. Each city had its local god or baal, which was worshipped at a high place either within the city or on some adjacent height, while in the larger cities elaborate altars and temples were reared to them. These local deities were regarded as the gods of fertility which gave to their worshippers ample harvests and numerous offspring both of the family and of the nock. The principle of generation occupied such a prominent place in the Canaanite cults that in time they became exceedingly immoral and debasing. To secure the favor of their gods the Canaanites brought rich sacrifices to their altars and observed certain great annual festivals with ceremonies very similar to those later adopted by the Hebrews.

While the Canaanites were on a much higher plane of material civilization than the Hebrews, they ultimately fell a prey to those hardy invaders of the desert: (1) Because they were incapable of strong united action, and (2) because their civilization was corrupt and enervating. Courage and real patriotism were almost unknown to them even as early as the seventeenth century B.C., when the Egyptian king Thutmose III invaded the land of Palestine. Their strong walls and their superior military equipment, however, made their immediate conquest by the Hebrews impossible. This explains why the earliest account of the initial conquest, now found in Judges 1, is chiefly devoted to recounting the strong Canaanite cities which the Hebrews failed to conquer.

III.

THE CAPTURE OF THE OUTPOSTS OF PALESTINE.

In the light of our present knowledge of the Canaanite civilization it becomes evident why most of the early Hebrew conquests were in the south. The only large Canaanite city which they could conquer in the early days was Jericho. Recent excavations have also shown why later generations regarded its capture by the Hebrews as a miracle, although many modern interpreters hold that the early account does not imply that it was by supernatural means. Like most of the Canaanite cities, it was situated on a slightly rising eminence, close to the foothills that on the west rose abruptly to the central plateau of Canaan. Northward, eastward, and southward, extended for miles the level plain of the Jordan river, which plowed its way through its alluvial bed, six miles east of Jericho. Close by the site of the ancient city came the perennial waters of the Wady Kelt with which it was possible to irrigate its fields. Past the town ran the main highway from across the Jordan, along the northern side of the Wady Kelt, to join the great central highway that extended through the centre of Palestine. Jericho was, therefore, the key to the land of Canaan, and its capture was necessary if the Hebrews were to maintain their connection with their kinsmen east of the Jordan.

The ruins of the ancient Canaanite town rise between forty and fifty feet above the plain. It is an oblong mound containing altogether about twelve acres. The excavations have disclosed a large part of the encircling wall. It was a construction of excellent workmanship which still stands practically intact, testifying to the accuracy of the early Hebrew tradition. Its foundation is a wall of rubble sixteen feet high and six to eight feet thick, sloping inward. On the top of this foundation, which rested on the native rock, was built a supplemental wall of burnt brick six or seven feet in thickness and rising even now in its ruined condition on an average eight feet above the lower wall. Thus the original wall must have towered between twenty and thirty feet above the plain. At the northern end of the city stood the citadel, made of unburnt brick, three stories high. Even the stone staircase which led to the top is still intact.

According to these investigators the late tradition that these walls fell flat to the earth as the result of a miracle finds no confirmation in the ruins themselves. The older Hebrew account, however, in their judgment agrees perfectly with the evidence revealed by the spade of the excavator. In imagination it is easy to follow the perilous journey of the Hebrew spies and to appreciate the importance of the negotiations by which they secured the co-operation of Rahab and of the clan within Jericho which she represented. Later come the Hebrew hordes from across the Jordan bearing with them the ark which symbolized to them the presence of Jehovah, who had led them on to victory in many an early battle. Behind their impregnable walls the inhabitants of Jericho must have laughed scornfully at the desert host, that seemed utterly incapable of an effective attack or of a protracted siege. According to many modern interpreters the earliest Hebrew host marched silently about the Canaanite stronghold. At first the inhabitants of Jericho, accustomed to Arab strategy, undoubtedly held themselves ready for defence. When no attack came, their vigilance was gradually relaxed. At last on the seventh day, when conditions were favorable, at the preconcerted signal, a trumpet blast, the Hebrews rushed toward the walls, the gates were probably opened by their allies within the city, and Jericho was quickly captured. The method of attack recorded in the prophetic narrative was very similar to the strategy used a little later by the Hebrews in the capture of the smaller towns of Ai and Bethel. They are the methods still employed by the Bedouins in their attacks upon the outposts of Palestine.

The fierce nomadic instincts of these early Hebrew warriors are revealed by the fate which they visited upon Jericho and its inhabitants. The recent excavations confirm the Biblical testimony that for several centuries after its initial capture the ancient town was left a heap of ruins.

Its inhabitants were slain as a great sacrificial offering to Jehovah, whose true character as one who loves all mankind was first appreciated by the inspired prophets of a much later From the plain of Jericho two or three roads led up to the central plateau of Canaan. The main road along the Wady Kelt ran past the villages of Ai and Bethel. At most they were small towns and easily captured. Along this highway went the Hebrew tribes later known as the

Ephraimites and Manassites. The other roads led through the wilderness southwestward to the heart of Judah. The frontier town of Bezek, mentioned in the ancient narrative of Judges, has not yet been identified. The name is perhaps but a scribal corruption of Bethlehem or of Bethzur further to the south. The other towns ultimately captured by the southern tribes were Hebron, with its copious water supply, Debir to the southwest, and Arad and Hormah which lay on the borders of the South Country. The capture of these six or seven outposts represents the first stage in the conquest and settlement of Palestine. It was significant because it meant that the people from the wilderness had gained a foothold in the land where they ultimately found their home. It inaugurated Israel's pioneer period. The Hebrews were no longer homeless wanderers in the desert, nor sojourners in a foreign land. At this point Israel's history as a nation properly begins, although the complete union of the tribes was not consummated until nearly a century later.

IV.

WAYS BY WHICH THE ISRAELITES WON THEIR HOMES.

The impression conveyed by the later passages in the book of Joshua that the Hebrews within a period of seven years became complete masters of the land of Canaan is different from that made by the older records in Judges. These indicate that the process was gradual, extending through several generations. Except at two or three great crises, this conquest appears to have been peaceful rather than by the sword, a process of settlement and colonization rather than of capture. Today throughout many parts of Palestine one may still see, close to the cities, the black tents and the flocks of the Bedouin immigrants. In the days of the Hebrew settlement the Canaanites were largely confined to the fertile valleys. The uplands were still open to the men from the desert. Here the Hebrews pitched their tents and finally built their rude homes. In this more favorable environment their families and their flocks gradually increased until they began to encroach upon the territory already occupied by the older inhabitants. The resulting quarrels and differences were sometimes settled by the appeal to the sword; more frequently by alliances sealed by intermarriages. The early narrative in the ninth and tenth chapters of the book of Judges gives a vivid picture of the resulting condition: in the strong Canaanite city of Shechem, Hebrews and Canaanites had so far intermarried that Abimelech, a product of this intermarriage, succeeded his father Gideon as king of the first little Hebrew kingdom. At Shechem Hebrews and Canaanites also worshipped side by side in the common sanctuary, which was known as "the temple of Baal of the Covenant."

Under the pressure of the increased population certain of the Hebrew tribes migrated and seized new territory. Such a migration is vividly recorded in Judges 17 and 18. The little tribe of the Danites, finding the pressure of their kinsmen on the north and east and that of the Philistines on the west too strong, captured the Canaanite city of Laish at the foot of Mount Hermon and thus found a permanent home in the upper Jordan valley.

It was a cruel, barbarous age in which might was regarded as right. Thus, Ehud the Benjamite, who treacherously gained admittance to the presence of Eglon, secretly slew this Moabite oppressor of the Hebrews. This act instead of being condemned was regarded then and even by later generations as an example of courageous patriotism. Was his act justifiable? How would it be regarded in America to-day?

V.

DEBORAH'S RALLY OF THE HEBREWS.

The growing numbers and strength of the Israelites at last alarmed the Canaanites. A certain leader by the name of Sisera formed a coalition of the strong Canaanite cities encircling the Plain of Esdraelon. The centre of this coalition was the powerful city of Megiddo, the ruins of which on the south-western side of the plain still remain to testify to the natural strength of this ancient stronghold. The policy of the Canaanites was to keep the different Hebrew clans apart and thus prevent united action. In the words of the ancient song:

> In the days of Jael the highways were unused,
> And travellers walked by round-about paths.
> The rulers ceased in Israel;
> A shield was not seen in five cities
> Nor a spear among forty thousand.

The one who alone appears to have understood the crisis and to have been able to stir the Israelites to action was Deborah, the prophetess of the central tribe of Issachar. Israel's struggle for independence is graphically recorded in the ancient poem found in Judges 5. The later prose version of the incident, found in Judges 4, supplements the earlier poem. To a chief of a northern tribe of Napthali, a certain Barak, she turned as the natural leader in the struggle for independence. Together they sent out the summons to the different northern tribes. The southern tribes of Judah and Simeon were apparently ignored. The distant tribes of Asher, Dan and Reuben were engrossed in their local interests and failed to respond. The tribesmen who rallied forty thousand strong on the northern side of the Plain of Esdraelon represented the great central Hebrew clans. The ancient song, sung by the women as they met the returning warriors, makes it possible to reconstruct the battle scene. Through the broad valleys that lead into the Plain of Esdraelon from the north came the sinewy, unkempt, roughly clad and poorly equipped Hebrew tribesmen, each clan led by its local chief. They had "come up to the help of Jehovah against the mighty." Tribal patriotism, the memory of past grievances, the desire for plunder, and zeal for Jehovah the God who had led their forefathers through the wilderness into the land of Canaan, stirred their courage and fired them to deeds of valor. Well they chose their battlefield, out on the plain on the northern side of the muddy, sluggish river Kishon. On the slightly rising ground they faced the Canaanite warriors who came out across the plain from the city of Megiddo, six miles away. The Canaanites were armed with chariots and the best weapons that the early Semitic civilization could produce, but one thing they lacked,—courage, fired by religious zeal.

Again a striking natural phenomenon appears suddenly to have turned the tide of Israel's fortune. On the eve of battle a drenching thunderstorm seems to have swept across the alluvial plain transforming it into a morass and the sluggish Kishon into a rushing, unfordable river. In the words of the ancient triumphal ode:

> From heaven fought the stars,
> From their courses fought against Sisera.
> The river Kishon swept them away,
> The ancient river, the river Kishon.
> O my soul, march on with strength!
> Then did the horse-hoofs resound
> With the galloping, galloping of their steeds.

The Hebrew even brings out the sound of the sucking of the horses' hoofs in the soft mud. The storm not only gave to the Hebrews, who were on foot, a vast advantage, but it meant to them that Jehovah, whose chariot was the clouds, his weapons, the lightning, and who spoke through the thunders, was fighting in their behalf.

The victory was overwhelming. Sisera, the Canaanite leader, fled, but only to fall later, ignominiously slain by a woman. Henceforth the Canaanite cities of central Palestine were occupied by the Hebrews. The vanquished were either enslaved or absorbed in intermarriage. From them, however, the Hebrews learned skill in agriculture and received a heritage of art, ideas and customs that had been developed by the Canaanites for many centuries. How far was this heritage beneficial to the Hebrews? What temptations did it bring to them? Did it mark a step forward in their development? Were the early Hebrews a pure or a mixed race?

More important than the spoils and lands which fell to the Hebrews was the new demonstration of Jehovah's ability and willingness to deliver his people which they received in the battle beside Kishon. Throughout all of Israel's colonial period the chief force binding the scattered Hebrew tribes together was their faith in Jehovah. The victory greatly strengthened that faith and prepared the way for the closer union which was necessary before Israel could become a permanent force among the nations of the earth. The vision of what they had been able to achieve through united action never completely faded from the memory of the Hebrews. Their subsequent experiences also tended to revive this memory. Amidst the warring elements in Palestine a powerful nation was gradually taking form; in the school of hard experience it was learning the lessons that were fitting it for a large life.

VI.

THE FINAL STAGE IN THE MAKING OP THE HEBREW NATION.

The final stage in the evolution of Israel is recorded in the opening chapters of I Samuel and is best studied in detail in connection with the history of the nation at its zenith. We have studied the forces which made the nation. A brief summary will indicate the transition to the next period, that of the kingdom. The victory over the Canaanites gave the Hebrews possession of the land and left them free to coalesce into a united nation; but the centrifugal tribe spirit for a time proved the stronger. Under Gideon a beginning was made in kingdom making, but owing to the cruelty and inefficiency of his son Abimelech, the first Hebrew state lasted little more than a generation.

The compelling power that finally brought all the rival Hebrew tribes together under a common leader was the conquest of their territory by the warlike, ambitious Philistines. In inspiring the Benjamite chieftain Saul to deliver his countrymen in their hour of shame and peril, Samuel the prophet proved the true father of the Hebrew kingdom. Under the compulsion of common danger the Israelites not only followed Saul to victory, but also made him their king. From this time on Israel took its place among the nations of the earth.

During their formative period the Hebrews acquired many characteristics that they have retained throughout their history. From their early nomadic life they inherited physical strength, hardihood, adaptability even to the most unfavorable environment, courage, perseverance and that individual initiative and self-reliance which come from protracted struggles against seemingly insuperable odds. It was a harsh but thorough school in which the infant nation Israel was trained. Their life in the wilderness and in the period of settlement also developed an intense love for freedom and that democratic spirit that was the glory of Israel and the foundation of its political institutions.

People passing their time chiefly out of doors and enjoying the uplifting stimulus of an unfettered life in the open naturally acquire a feeling of awe and reverence for the God of nature that is often lacking in the city dweller. Especially is this true if, like the early Hebrews, the dwellers in the open feel that need of divine protection which is begotten by constant exposure to danger, hunger, hardship and hostile foes. The many crises and the signal deliverances that came to the Hebrews not only intensified their faith, but also gave them the consciousness that the God in whom they put their trust was both able and eager to deliver them. Prophets like Moses strengthened the popular sense of Jehovah's immediate presence and interpreted the significance of each event.

Israel's early faith was simple, like that of a little child. While its beliefs were crude, its trust was strong. It was this trust and loyalty that carried the child nation through its early crises and ultimately bound together the separate tribes into a united commonwealth. Thus Israel's early history illustrates the fundamental truth, that the most essential, the most powerful force in the making of a nation is a simple, practical, every-day religion.

Questions for Further Consideration.

Should the successful and easy crossing of the Jordan by the Israelites be ascribed to miracle or to their own promptness in seizing an opportunity unexpectedly offered?

In what ways did the religious zeal of the ancient Hebrews in battle differ from the fanatical zeal of the modern Moslem in fighting the Christians? Or the zeal of the Japanese before Port Arthur?

When, if ever, is assassination justifiable as a political expedient? Give your reasons.

Were the Hebrews justified in the methods employed in securing control of Palestine?

Is it right for a progressive nation to compel a backward nation to submit? Were the Americans on this ground justified in seizing the lands of the Indians?

What were the chief tenets in the early faith of the Hebrews?

How did Israel's faith affect its political development?

In what important ways was religion effective in making the English state? The American commonwealth?

Subjects for Further Study.

(1) The Structure and Literary History of the Book of Judges, McFadyen, *Introd. to O. T.* 76-83; Kent, *Student's O. T.* I, 26, 27.
(2) Conditions in Canaan at the Time of the Hebrew Settlement. Paton, *Early Hist. of Syria and Pal.*, 157-60; Maspero, *Struggle of the Nations*, 111-208; *Encyc. Bib.* II, 2223-5.
(3) The Motives that Inspired the Leaders of the American Revolution. Fiske, Lodge, Bancroft or other writers on this period.

BIBLIOBAZAAR

The essential book market!

Did you know that you can get any of our titles in large print?

Did you know that we have an ever-growing collection of books in many languages?

Order online:
www.bibliobazaar.com

Find all of your favorite classic books!

Stay up to date with the latest government reports!

At BiblioBazaar, we aim to make knowledge more accessible by making thousands of titles available to you- *quickly and affordably*.

Contact us:
BiblioBazaar
PO Box 21206
Charleston, SC 29413

Printed in the United States
116053LV00001B/27/A